Shadows
in the
Curtain

Cami Checketts

Shadows

in the

Curtain

Cami Checketts

Shadows in the Curtain

Cover Art by Sherry Gammon
Cover Copyright Camille Coats Checketts
Interior Design by Heather Justesen

Birch River Publishing

Published in the United States of America

Dedication

To my husband. Thank you for being my sizzle and my comfort. I'll love you forever.

Acknowledgments

Thank you to Sherry Gammon for designing my beautiful cover, Sadie Anderson for editing, and Heather Justesen for type-setting.

Thank you to all my fabulous critique partners: Sherry Gammon, Cindy Anderson, Amanda Tru, Daniel Coleman, Eric Bishop, and Christina Dymock.

Chapter One

EMMALINE SQUINTED INTO THE BRIGHT LIGHTS, focusing on the exuberant crowd instead of ignoring them as she had throughout the night. She bowed and smiled, exhausted but thrilled with the performance. Many, most particularly her aunt, would say her current situation was beneath her abilities. The dilapidated Coaster Theater in Cannon Beach, Oregon may not be the most glamorous venue, but the people she worked with were sincere in their understated talent and she found playing narrator in *Joseph and the Technicolor Dream Coat* was always a challenge.

A young girl ran to Emmy and presented her with a huge bouquet of red roses. Emmy bent and hugged the child before holding the bouquet aloft. The crowd bellowed their approval.

As she lowered the flowers, Emmy saw the note. She swallowed hard, swaying slightly. Timothy, who played the part of Joseph, rested a hand on her back.

"You okay?" he asked through his smile, waving to the crowd.

She pulled the flowers to where he could see the note. *You're Mine*, written in bold permanent marker on a cut piece of blue cardstock. An exact replica of the other notes.

1

Timothy's hand gripped her waist possessively. If it would've been anyone else, she would've told him to back off, she was married, but Timothy was a close friend and his protection like a brother's. "Stay close to me," he said.

They exited the stage and hurried down the hallway. The rest of the cast trailed behind, feet tapping loudly on the concrete floor as they rushed to the front foyer to greet their fans.

The director and prop manager stood in the hallway congratulating the cast. The director, James, every inch a gentleman from his pressed vest to his bowtie, gave her a slight bow. Emmy adored the older man. The prop manager, Shane, grinned shyly at Emmy and squeezed her hand. He looked rough with his unkempt beard and dark, scraggly hair, but his kindness endeared him to the cast.

Her husband, Grayson, ducked through the doorway leading into the front hallway, a bright spot against the dingy paint. "You were unreal, Em."

She handed him the flowers, hoping he'd see the note and know what to do. He bent and gave her a quick kiss before she was swept passed him to the waiting throng.

"I'll be here," he called.

Emmy wished she could stay with him and let him protect her, but she couldn't neglect her supporters. Many of these people attended performance after performance, and although her fake gaiety hid mounting fear and frustration, they deserved to at least shake her hand and receive a smile.

Timothy stuck to her side while people surged passed with compliments, hand squeezes, and the occasional hug. Emmy searched every eye, but only saw excitement from a fun performance or weariness from sitting too long. If anyone had murder in mind, he was as good at putting on a fake face as she was.

No one piqued her curiosity. Until he came. She had no clue what his name was, but the past few weeks she'd seen him almost every morning at the gym. He was much too good-looking, with his rippling muscles and deep blue eyes. She always avoided looking directly at him, though she knew that was as obvious an indicator of her attraction as staring would be. She couldn't avoid him now.

The wide entryway, which featured plush, faded carpet and wood-planked walls, shrank as he drew nearer. The babble of the crowd faded. He reached for her hand, staring deep into her eyes. Her hand fitted itself into his like he was a magnet. Her entire body leaned toward him.

"You were amazing. So passionate." He smiled and the room swayed.

Emmy was quite sure the passion she experienced right now had nothing to do with singing or acting. She should draw away but couldn't force herself to. "Thank you," she managed, embarrassed by the huskiness of her voice as she tried to catch a breath.

The crowd pressed forward, and he was forced to release her hand and move to the side. His blonde date gushed over Emmy for a second, and then they were gone.

Emmy continued greeting other patrons but couldn't forget the allure of his blue eyes. He didn't seem like the creepy stalker type, but she had to wonder. Could he be the one sending the notes?

The last of the crowd finally filtered out the doors. Emmy congratulated her fellow cast members and accepted their praise. She looked up to see her husband leaning against the refreshment counter with a warm smile on his face, brown hair flopping into his right eye.

Heat rushed to her cheeks. She'd allowed herself to react to another man. She was stronger than that. Trained to project emotions on demand, she was also an expert at reining in any untoward feelings and separating herself from her role, no matter how attractive her co-star may be. Why had she let her guard down tonight? It must be because of her fear over another note or maybe seeing that man in a different environment.

Whatever it was, it wouldn't happen again. Grayson reached her side and bent to kiss her. His kiss was sure and steady. Maybe not exciting or passionate, but filled with love and the only home she knew. Grayson was hot cocoa and a fire on a chilly Oregon night.

"Emmy," her husband almost growled her name. His normally serene green eyes flashed. "The police will be here soon. We'll find out who's sending these notes."

Emmy wilted against his lanky frame. She didn't doubt the police would try, but it had been months. She wished her stalker would either show his face and give her a chance to smack him good or leave her alone.

Chapter Two

EMMALINE PRETENDED SHE DIDN'T FEEL his eyes on her as she strode to the leg press. It didn't matter where she was in the gym, he discreetly watched. She was flattered, but married. Although a beautiful distraction, she couldn't allow herself to be taken in by him.

She should've done one more set of rows, but she had to get out of there—get away from those blue eyes and back to the reality of the man she loved, the man she'd pledged her life to.

Emmy grabbed her keys and jacket from the shelves by the door and reached for the handle, mumbling a thank you to the attendant. The door burst open from the outside; two teenagers scurried through. Emmy was knocked to the side and lost her balance. A pair of strong arms wrapped around her from behind, catching her. She found her footing, whirled in the man's embrace, and looked into pools of blue, sparkling like the ocean in Tahiti.

Her mouth hung open. Besides their exchange after *Joseph* several weeks ago, she'd kept her distance. She'd forced herself to forget those eyes with brown lashes longer than any woman's, the strong jaw line and slightly hollowed cheeks that had slight dimples in them when he smiled—which he was doing right now.

"Are you okay, Sweetheart?"

Her lips compressed. She was nobody's sweetheart but Grayson's. Emmy pulled free of his grasp. Risking one more glance into those eyes, she realized she needed to wipe the dimples from his face before she tripped on purpose so he'd catch her again.

"Tell me you have a beautiful wife and at least two adorable children at home and you're just smiling at me because you're an incredibly nice guy who has no agenda where I'm concerned."

Dimples erased.

He exhaled slowly, eyes darkening like a storm blowing in. "No wife and no adorable children."

Emmy folded her arms across her chest. To his credit his eyes didn't rove from hers, but when she thought about it, they never did. Every time she caught his gaze on her, he was looking at her face, not her body.

"Yeah, well, I do," she said. "Awesome husband, that is, and he wouldn't appreciate the way you're always checking me out."

He didn't look away, nor did he deny it. He brushed a hand through his longish sandy-blond hair before nodding slowly. "You're right. I, um, never noticed a ring or had the guts to talk to you before now. Now that I know you're married," he swallowed, "I won't bother you again."

Something inside her melted at the sad look in his eyes and his admission that he hadn't dared approach her and wouldn't have even been looking if she'd worn her ring. It was just obnoxiously huge and rubbed against her finger when she lifted weights. She'd buy a gold band today.

"Thanks." For some reason, she wanted to reassure him,

maybe bring back one of the dimples. She forced a smile. "No worries for you, since every other woman in Cannon Beach is after you." Did that sound as awkward to him as it did to her?

He frowned and held the door open for her. She nodded to him before slinking through the door and could've sworn he said, "But not the right woman."

Waves softly crashed on the beach a hundred feet from their home. Emmy leaned on the deck railing, soaking up the new day, the salt in the air, her wet hair dampening her shirt, and the sun warming her forehead. She only had fifteen minutes to dry her dark hair, put some makeup on, and eat breakfast before her first voice student showed up, but she wanted to sit and watch the ocean, go on a walk, or better yet, take a long swim.

Grayson came up behind her, resting his chin on top of her head. She smiled at the feel of his tall, gangly body wrapped around her. He was so comfortable to lean against. They'd spent their teenage years as neighbors and best friends. Grayson had pursued her for years before she agreed to marry him. Then he'd moved her away from the craziness of L.A. and the theater crowd who would trample anyone to be on top. Now, she acted at a lesser theater with people she adored, taught music to sweet children, and loved every minute with her husband. With the exception of the disturbing notes, the past year had been the most content and peaceful time of her life.

"You want to go swimming?" he guessed.

She sighed. "Yes, but I've got a student coming any

minute and I'm sure you have a lot of work to do."

He kissed her hair. "I'll watch you when I get home." The software company he worked for in Portland let him set his own hours and work from home on occasion, but he still was gone more than she liked.

"Thanks," she said. "That would be great."

Grayson assumed she would give up swimming in the ocean when they'd moved to the cooler waters of Oregon. She argued that with a full-length wetsuit, she was as warm as she'd been in California. He'd finally played the petrified husband card and made her swear to only swim if he came with her or watched from the beach. She didn't doubt his love, but sometimes she felt smothered. Her acting career was just like her swimming. He'd come to every practice and performance since the threatening notes began. If he realized men were hitting on her at the gym, he'd get a membership tomorrow.

He pressed a soft kiss to her lips. As always, Emmy hoped for passion to ignite within her at his kiss. As always, it was pleasant and short.

She glanced back at the beach and saw the man from the gym. Swallowing, she forced herself not to react. *What is he doing here?* He met her gaze.

She drew a couple of shaky breaths before turning and focusing on her husband.

The ringing phone gave her an excuse to go inside.

"Drive safe," Emmy said to Grayson as she walked into their two-story living room and reached for the cordless on the coffee table.

"Love you." Grayson closed the sliding glass door and then left through the garage entrance off the laundry room.

"Love you too." She pushed the button on the phone. "Hello."

"Emmaline," Aunt Jalina's voice screeched in her ear. "I read some wonderful reviews about your performance in *Joseph*. I'd be proud if you were actually performing with a company worth being called a company."

"Good morning, Auntie." Emmy shook her head. Aunt Jalina sounded in good spirits.

"It's an awful morning. When are you going to come home or at least make that skinny husband of yours move you to Portland so you can perform with a respectable group?"

"And give up this view?" Emmy paused and smiled at the truth of her statement. Two-story windows showcased waves crashing on the beach. Haystack Rock decorated the background. "Not a chance. How's Uncle Carl?"

"Happy as ever—sends you his love."

Emmy smiled. At least she knew that her uncle loved her. Her aunt did in her own twisted way, but sometimes it was hard to feel through the criticism. "Give him a kiss for me. I've got to run; students are on their way."

"Students? You waste your abilities teaching children who could never rise to the talent and training you've been blessed with."

Emmy walked into the kitchen and put some bread in the toaster. "Oh, I don't know about that. I've got some very promising children here."

"Pshaw. You may think it's fun to tease me, Emmaline, but your mother would be rolling over in her grave."

Emmy clutched the butter knife in her hand. "Now that's where you're wrong, Auntie, my mother was proud of me no matter what."

"Your mother was proud because you were a success! What are you now? A twenty-five year old who's already washed up and given up."

Emmy stood to her full 5'6". She knew all her mother would've wanted was her happiness. "I am successful at what I'm doing. I'm happy and respected here. I'd never go back to that cesspool of cutthroats."

Jalina clucked her tongue. "Darling, I know you didn't enjoy L.A. I'm not saying you have to move back here, but please consider auditioning in Portland at least."

"Did I not speak clearly? I am happy here."

"Don't you get uppity with me! If you don't do something with your life..." She paused, then continued with her shrill voice. "I will cut you out of my inheritance."

Emmy laughed at that. "Oh, Auntie, when has money ever been a motivator for me?"

"It should be! You know how horrible it is to go without."

Emmy's young life had been filled with want as her mother earned just enough to survive. Somehow there had always been money for Emmy's acting, vocal, and piano lessons. She'd been too young and loved the lessons too much to question why they didn't have enough food but could afford the best private tutors. "Don't pretend you don't feel guilty about that," Emmy said.

"If your mother wouldn't have lied to us all those years. She would only let me pay for your lessons. I had no clue."

She didn't go on and Emmy was grateful. Her aunt and uncle were devastated when they'd finally forced her mother to let them visit her dilapidated Chicago apartment. They saw for themselves that Emmy's mother could barely afford rent and food, living off a waitress' salary after Emmy's father deserted them. Uncle Carl and Aunt Jalina moved them to Glendora, California and spoiled them both until her mother died three years ago from the cancer that ate away her breasts and then her vital organs. Even though she'd been twenty-one, Emmy hadn't been prepared to lose her mom. She missed her mother's quiet and unfailing love.

Her aunt insisted Emmy finish her M.F.A. from American Conservatory Theater in San Francisco before auditioning with the best companies in L.A. At twenty-four she had been an acclaimed performer, but miserable. She had no hope of rescue until Grayson talked her into marrying him and moved her away from it all.

A loud rap came from the sliding glass door.

"I've got a student here, Auntie." Emmy hung up without waiting for goodbye and motioned to her next door neighbor to come in. "Student" was a loose term to use—she considered Kelton and his family her closest friends.

Kelton's white teeth split his copper skin as he thrust the back door open. "How's the prettiest voice teacher in Cannon Beach?"

"*Only* voice teacher in Cannon Beach." Emmy rolled her eyes. "I'll be better when I hear you practiced every day this week."

"Ha. We both know I only take lessons so I can come visit you and keep my momma from kicking me in the butt." The brawny defender for Seaside High's lacrosse team made it clear that hitting the gym and flirting with girls were more important than developing his musical ability.

Emmy shook her head, hiding a smile at his usual antics. The boy was inappropriate, but she loved him like the nephew she'd never had. "We're both going to kick your behind if you

11

don't start practicing."

Kelton shrugged innocently and made his way to the piano. Emmy forgot about missing breakfast, her aunt, and the man from the gym as she played the piano and encouraged her uncommitted yet talented neighbor.

Chapter Three

JOSH PLODDED THROUGH THE SOFT SAND of Cannon Beach. He'd already lifted this morning, but he needed a bit more exertion to clear his mind. Exercise had helped him overcome depression after his divorce, but it was failing him today.

The temperature hovered close to seventy, one of those rare hours without rain. A perfect July day and the first day in weeks he wasn't at the fire station or on call. He wanted to enjoy it, but the encounter at the gym this morning had spoiled any chance of that.

The majestic Haystack Rock jutted out of the ocean, and waves softly rolled over the sand. Most beach-goers soaked up the fleeting sunshine and fixated on the scenery; Josh sprinted until he almost couldn't hear her voice in his head, "Please tell me you have a beautiful wife and two adorable children at home." His legs and lungs burned. Though he didn't want to quit, his muscles gave out, and he was forced to slow. He stopped to stretch, focusing on the water.

Why couldn't he get her out of his head? No matter how pretty she was, how nice she seemed, how drawn he felt to her, she was married. He thought his life ended when his wife cheated on him. He would never do that to someone else. Never.

He glanced from the endless waves of the ocean to the beautiful homes dotting the beach. The sun crested the rooftops of the homes to the east. Squinting against the glare, he wondered if his mind was playing tricks on him. But no, it was her, standing on a huge deck. She stared at the water, her mahogany hair wet and trailing over one shoulder.

The sliding glass door behind her opened and a tall man strode across the patio and wrapped his arms around her.

Josh groaned. *What am I doing?* He wasn't a stalker or some teenager with a crush. He looked away from the happy couple, picked up a rock, and hurled it into the ocean. Why did she have to be married? The humidity chilled him even though the sun tried to help. Was it the humidity or his own guilt? After his divorce, he'd promised himself to be extremely picky about which women he became involved with.

Relocating from Boise, Idaho to this small town in Oregon had been perfect, until he saw the brunette in the gym. He'd watched from afar and attempted to ignore the attraction, trying to protect his heart from another injury.

He couldn't stop himself from falling when he saw her perform at the Coaster Theater. He'd heard the phrase, "own the stage", but never really knew what it meant until he watched her that night. Her voice and the way she moved captivated him. He might as well have told his date he was sorry for wasting her time, stood in the crowded theater, and declared his intentions to pursue Emmaline. Since then he'd waited for the perfect opportunity to approach her. An hour ago she'd ruined every plan he'd made. Married.

He turned and allowed himself one more look. She met his gaze briefly before breaking away from her husband and slipping back into the house. He wasn't sure if she'd recognized him or not; she hadn't given any indication if she had. He hoped not. She'd probably think he was following her.

Out of the corner of his eye, he noticed a man staring in the exact direction he was. The man was close to Josh's six-two, had on a baseball hat and sunglasses, and was scrunched down into a windbreaker so Josh couldn't distinguish anything about his features but a straight nose.

The man noticed him, dipped his head, and sauntered off. Josh wondered if the guy had been watching the woman too, or if he was just overanalyzing everything because he felt like a stalker himself right now.

He pivoted and pushed off the sand. Looked like he'd be sprinting, again.

Chapter Four

EMMY AND GRAYSON SHARED AN EXHILARATING late-afternoon swim, showered, and then ate one of Emmy's creations. Grayson always teased that her dinners were either tantalizing or so nasty they had to scrape the food in the garbage and order takeout. Tonight Emmy had followed part of a recipe, only improvising on a few ingredients, and the shrimp scampi was delicious. She relished nights like this: no lingering deadlines for Grayson's software company, no rehearsals, no one but the two of them.

"Do you mind if I watch the PGA tour?" Grayson asked.

Golf—the epitome of boredom on television. "No. I'll bring a book down and sit with you."

"Hate to bore you." He winked.

"Maybe you could give me attention during commercials."

"DVR. I'll fast-forward commercials." He grinned, teasing as usual.

"And the romance is dead." Emmy laughed, hoping he didn't see that it bothered her.

"And after only a year. We'll be in trouble by our twenty-year anniversary." Grayson gave her a one-arm hug, clutching a Mountain Dew in his other palm, before heading down to the basement theater room.

Emmy sighed, frustrated but at the same time grateful that Grayson didn't suspect her disappointment in their ho-hum love life. Things were comfortable and she was happy. Maybe sizzle was too much to ask. She glanced out the window at the dark beach beyond. She never closed the blinds, but tonight she thought about it. Even with Grayson here, she felt really alone.

She finished scrubbing the granite countertop and sweeping the tile, then ran up to their bedroom to get her Kindle. She downloaded the latest Sherry Gammon novel. A door opened and closed on the main level. Weird. Was Grayson going outside? She couldn't imagine him pausing his beloved golf championship, especially when he already had a Mountain Dew in hand.

Opening the book with her fingertip, Emmy scrolled through the pages and read the first line. *Madeline knew she had to kill him or she'd never be free.* Hmm. Could be interesting or morbid. At least she knew one of her favorite authors would entertain her and have a hero she could drool about.

Before losing herself in the new book, she descended the sweeping staircase to the main floor and then the narrower set to the basement. The commentator whispered about a bogey ruining someone's chances. Grayson had the volume up. Emmy shook her head. Only Grayson would care to hear what the announcer said. She couldn't get into golf in real life let alone on television. Last time they'd played, she'd hit Grayson's ball into the pond, supposedly a huge faux pas.

"Think you've got it loud enough?" she asked as she rounded the doorway.

Blood ran down Grayson's shirt and splattered the

leather sofa and side tables. Emmy dropped her Kindle. A scream ripped from her throat as she ran to Grayson's side.

Though his head slumped to the side, he was upright, remote in hand, like he was actually watching the television.

The screams kept coming. She couldn't think. She wanted to help him, to stuff all that blood back into his body and make him be okay. Staring at him, tears ran down her face as horrendous shrieks came from her throat.

She forced herself to press her fingers to his neck. Bile rose in her throat at all the blood. Grayson's blood. She said a quick prayer, *Please let him live.*

Even as she searched for a pulse she knew he was gone. Her best friend. Her husband. *Maybe there's a pulse and I just can't feel it.* This thin thread of hope calmed her down enough to pick up the cordless on the side table, dial 911, and cry into the phone. "Husband. Stabbed. Help!"

Josh hadn't enjoyed his day off as much as he should, and after flipping through a few television channels tonight, he found himself walking on the same stretch of beach as this morning. He ran a hand through his hair, trying to convince himself he was just out for a walk on the beach closest to his house, and not becoming more obsessed with a married woman. But the guy watching her house this morning bugged him. He wanted to make sure that guy didn't come back. At least that's what he told himself.

Sirens ruptured the peace of waves crashing against the sand. Red and blue light radiated into the night sky. When the lights converged on her house, Josh didn't stop to think.

Sand filled his shoes as he ran. He sprinted around the front and into the house, banging through the tall wooden door. Kaden, a young deputy, almost ran into him.

"Hey, Campbell." Kaden looked over his shoulder. "Where's the fire truck?"

"I'm not on duty. What happened?" Josh's gut clenched tight. Please let her be okay. What if something happened to her?

"Wife found the husband stabbed."

"The wife?"

"Head case. She insists we take him to the hospital, but it's an obvious DOA. Housley's making sure we've got an all clear. You want to try to talk her into getting away from the body so we can get some evidence? The EMTs should be here any second."

This was one of the things Josh loved about this small town police squad. They were too relaxed, but they were also willing to accept help rather than put a barrier between the different departments. "Where is she?"

Kaden pointed down. Josh rushed through the huge foyer and took the stairs two at a time. He sensed her sobbing before he actually heard it. The scene was surreal, ugly and more sickening than anyone should have to live through. The man had been stabbed multiple times, blood spattered the furniture. The beautiful woman from his every thought lay with her dark hair buried in her husband's shoulder, crying like her world had ended. It probably had.

Josh felt for a pulse, nothing. She didn't seem to notice he was there until he touched her shoulder. "Ma'am?"

Emmaline slowly turned and looked at him. Her mouth dropped open for a minute then fire shot from her gaze as she leaped to her feet and slapped him in the face. Josh reeled back. She came at him with claws drawn like a momma cat protecting its kittens. Josh secured both of her hands with one of his and wrapped his other arm around her back to calm her down. She was so small he could've covered her entire back and abdomen with one arm.

"You," she screamed, struggling to break from his grasp. "How dare you come here!"

"Please, ma'am, calm down."

"Don't tell me to calm down, you murderer!"

Murderer? She must be so upset. The poor confused woman. "I'm very sorry about your husband."

"I'll bet you are." Emmaline drew back her head and actually tried to ram him. Josh deflected the blow, but unfortunately allowed one of her hands to get free and she started hitting him again.

"Campbell?" Housley rushed into the room. "Need some help?"

"No." Josh restrained her hands. Housley stood close by, ready to assist.

"I'm with the fire department," Josh said. "I know the police will do everything in their power to apprehend the person responsible and I will try to help anyway I can."

"Yeah right, you will! I told you I was married and you just couldn't take that, could you?" She half-turned and looked at her husband. "Did you think after you murdered him that I would come running to you?"

"I, murdered..." She really did think he'd killed her husband. Josh released her, stunned. Thankfully she stood there like she'd been horse-whipped and didn't try to pummel him again. "Why would you think I murdered your husband?"

Emmaline swallowed. Her dark eyes sparkled with

wetness. "The notes."

"What notes?" Josh felt as if he were watching a television show, like this couldn't possibly be reality and he could just turn it off and walk away. It was then he noticed Kaden had entered the room and both he and Housley were eyeing him like they weren't sure what they were watching either. Men that trusted and respected him, looking at him like they thought this woman might not be insane.

Housley held up a plastic sack with a quarter sheet of paper in it. Written boldly on blue cardstock were the words, "*Now we can be together.*"

"She's been receiving notes for a few months now. Jamison and I have documented everything."

"I had no idea."

Housley shrugged. "The perp never did anything, until..." He glanced at the body and reddened.

"The other notes all came to the opera house," she cut in, glaring at Josh and ignoring everyone else. "You were there the night I got the last one."

Josh swallowed several times before trusting himself to answer. "You can't think because of what happened this morning." He focused on her tortured brown eyes.

She folded her arms underneath her chest. "What would you think?"

Josh shook his head, raking his fingers through his hair. "I promise you I would never harm your husband so I could have a chance with you."

She just stared at him. "Get out of my house!" Her lip trembled and tears rolled through her dark lashes.

"But, you can't believe..." He reached out a hand to reassure her, but her icy stare froze more than his hand in

21

place.

"Campbell." Kaden tugged at his arm. "Why don't you go upstairs while we help Mrs. Henderson?"

Josh blinked at him. Did they believe *her*?

"I think it would help everyone calm down." He glanced at Emmaline before looking back to Josh.

"Fine." Josh pulled his arm away. He looked at Emmaline one more time as she stood there defiantly glowering at him. The only sign of her trauma were the tears that trailed silently down her cheeks.

"I know you have no reason to trust me," he said, "but I'll help the police in any way I can and someday you'll know that I would never put you through this kind of pain."

Fire shot from her eyes. "You have no idea what kind of pain I'm in and *nothing* you do will make it better."

Chapter Five

One Year Later

THE GROCERY STORE. It was a unique form of torture for Emmy. She used to be in her element picking out delicious produce and meats, envisioning the food she could create. Now she had no one to cook for, and it was the curse of living in a small town that she always ran into someone who knew her gruesome story. The pity in their eyes ruined what was once an enjoyable experience.

The theater was different. Her fellow actors resided in their character's heads, and she was completely happy to pretend to be someone else when she was with them. Those who attended the theater saw the mask she wore and accepted it. They'd moved passed the oozing compassion stage. But the rest of the Cannon Beach populace handed pity to her like a neighbor bringing cookies—well-meaning but still going to make you squishy if you take it all in.

She lifted a gala apple to check for bruises, already anticipating the crunchy sweetness.

"Oh, Emmy, you pretty little thing."

Mrs. Baxter. Not now.

Emmy forced a smile, meeting the lady's age-clouded eyes. The eyes were always the hardest thing to focus on, but she couldn't allow herself to be a wimp.

"Hello, Mrs. Baxter. How's your new grandson?"

The woman's blue-veined hand reached out to grasp Emmy's forearm as she leaned closer. "He's fat and beautiful, but it's you I'm concerned about. How are you holding up, my darling?"

"Wonderful." Emmy felt a twinge of guilt. People always meant well. She pretended she was on stage and gave the older woman a smile so bright, it should've made Mrs. Baxter shield her eyes.

"Now don't you lie to me." Mrs. Baxter tightened her grip until it was almost painful. "I've lost my lover and I know the agony of being alone."

Emmy had heard the "lost lover" story dozens of times. She couldn't handle it today. "Thank you for being so understanding." She tugged her arm free and gripped her shopping cart. Crisp apples would have to wait. "I've got to run. A student will be at my house soon."

She pushed the cart away, the woman's final words bouncing off her back. "It will get better!"

Emmy cringed. It had been a year. Nothing had gotten better.

It was an accomplishment to make it to the store or take a shower. The only reason she got out of bed were her students and the theater.

Crash! Her cart came to an abrupt halt as she rounded the corner and slammed into another patron's grocery cart. The impact knocked her off balance, propelling her sideways into a cereal display. Boxes of cereal dumped around her feet.

"Sorry, I didn't see you." A large hand wrapped around her waist and lifted her out of the mess.

"Thank you." Emmy turned to look into startling blue

24

eyes. Oh, no. *Him.* Captain Joshua Campbell. Firefighter extraordinaire. Town goldenboy. Wasn't Mrs. Baxter enough punishment for one day?

She bent and retrieved several boxes of Cheerios, praying he'd go away. But no, always the gentleman, he grabbed the Lucky Charms and helped her fix the display. It was impossible not to run into each other in this small town, and she'd observed him doing everything from comforting a toddler who had dropped his ice cream cone to changing tires for people stranded on the highway. He was just one of those who were too good to be true and it fueled her anger and cynicism. She recognized that blaming him for Grayson's death was unreasonable, but he almost brought it on himself—always worrying about her, promising he'd find the murderer. She'd finally accepted the evidence that he couldn't be the murderer, but she still felt guilty for her feelings of attraction toward Josh before Grayson died. She wanted nothing to do with him.

Thankfully he didn't say anything while they worked side by side, curious shoppers gawking as they walked passed. The air between them was charged like static electricity. Emmy checked to see if her hair stood on end. She hated the awareness she always felt when he appeared. Even though she kept trying to convince herself she wanted nothing to do with him, it was like her body had different ideas. The cereal was organized much too quickly.

She clutched her shopping cart handle and pushed off, ordering her body to forget about it.

His hand on her arm stopped the forward momentum and made her shiver at the pleasant sensation.

"How are you?"

She'd been so proud of herself earlier for meeting Mrs. Baxter's gaze. She couldn't do it with Josh. She studied his chin and unfortunately found herself wondering if the stubble would be rough or soft. It looked long enough to be soft and she loved the way it shadowed his face.

No! Stop noticing him.

"It's really none of your business how I am." Her voice could've cooled hot chocolate.

His hand dropped from her arm. She should've felt relief instead of remorse at the loss of his touch.

"Um, I know that," he said. "I just...worry about you."

That did it. Her head snapped up and she was able to meet those blue eyes without wanting to melt. "You and everybody else in this town! I. Am. Fine." She glanced around at several other people she knew, glowering until they resumed their shopping. Except for Mrs. Baxter, who just gave her that compassionate smile.

Emmy turned back to Josh. "Fine. No one needs to worry about me. Especially *you*." She poked him in the chest and jammed her finger on the hard musculature. She bit down on the yelp that wanted to escape, ignored his whipped puppy look, and shoved her shopping cart away. He was the last person on earth who needed to worry about her.

Chapter Six

KELTON BANGED ON THE SLIDING GLASS DOOR. Emmy managed a weak smile, staring at him through bleary eyes but not standing up from the couch. Last night had been a bad one. Even with the expensive security system she'd installed, she had trouble sleeping and cowered at every creak. She'd finally turned on her white noise machine to shut out the little sounds, but then she stayed awake wondering if the device drowned out the approach of the murderer. The notes had stopped after Grayson's death, and although the murderer seemed to have disappeared from everywhere but her nightmares, she realized her fears had only grown.

"How's the prettiest voice teacher in Cannon Beach?"

"Tired." Too tired to reprimand him for his standard flirtation.

"Seriously, you look like crap." He flopped his brawny frame into the overstuffed chair.

"Ouch. So your opening line is just to make me feel good?"

He grinned. "You're still beautiful. You just look like you haven't slept." He paused, studying her. "Doing okay?"

"Yeah. It's just..." For some reason she couldn't formulate the standard lies today. *I'm fine. I'm doing better.* The sincere look in Kelton's eyes almost made her cry. Under all the teasing, he was a great kid. Kelton's family and her fellow actors at the theater were the only friends she could claim anymore. Grayson had been her best friend; no one filled that role.

"Just sucks. I know." He rubbed his large palms on the chair's arms. "I think it's chill you stayed here and didn't move back to L.A. like your crazy aunt wanted you to."

Emmy had endured days of fighting with her aunt, including an embarrassing feud during the funeral dinner, before she convinced Jalina that she wasn't leaving the home she and Grayson had been so happy in, her students, or her theater.

"I couldn't leave my house."

He frowned.

"Or my favorite neighbors." Kelton and his family were wonderful to her.

That brought a smile back. "Or the Coaster Theater. People would *flip*." He drawled the word out. "You're such a superstar."

She didn't need to be a superstar, but she would do anything for the theater. "I love it there. The theater and my students are the only reason I get out of bed in the morning." *Wow, I really am pathetic.*

"I know one student in particular." He grinned. "I can totally take it that you have a huge thing for me. It's chill. And now you don't have to think of me as jailbait."

She arched her eyebrows, shaking her head at his lingo. "*Jailbait?*"

"Yeah, you know, I turn eighteen next month."

"Kelton!" Emmy sputtered. "You're not really trying to

28

say..."

"No, no, I was just joking." He held up his hands. "But if, you know, you're ever ready." He shrugged. "Just thought I'd put it out there."

"I barely lost my husband, I'm eight years older than you, *and* your teacher." She cringed as she said "barely". It would be a year next week since Grayson's murder, and many people thought she should be ready to move on—Aunt Jalina being the most vocal.

He clucked his tongue. "Yeah, there is that. Okay. This conversation just," he made a dive-bomb motion with his hands, "got heavy." He jumped to his feet. "Why don't you swim anymore?"

Emmy swallowed. She'd almost prefer his insinuations. Kelton always teased, but he was harmless and had been there for her the past year. He was one of the few people she could be honest with, an easygoing teenager who didn't read something into everything she said. "It always worried Grayson, and I feel guilty..." She didn't finish with the "enjoying myself", but rather looked out at the ocean, which was bluish gray on this misty July day.

"No lesson today. We're swimming."

Emmy stared at him. "You can't call off the lesson. I'm the teacher."

"I know, you *always* remind me." He winked. "But you need to do something for you. I'll freeze my butt off in that ocean to prove I'm your friend."

Emmy only hesitated for half a minute before saying, "I'll meet you at the beach."

Kelton grinned. "Hopefully you can keep up with me."

❧

Emmy swam every day over the next couple of weeks, a few times with Kelton and his twelve-year old twin brothers, most of the time alone. It was so liberating. She was her former carefree self in the water. No worries about some freak appearing to stab her like they'd stabbed Grayson. No anguish over missing her husband. No guilt over sometimes forgetting how wonderful he had been.

She didn't have rehearsal tonight and decided to go for an evening swim. It was raining, but that was normal and wouldn't bother her in the water. Donning a full-length wetsuit, it only took a few minutes for her body to acclimatize to the water temperature. She let her thoughts run as her arms and legs sliced through the water. Her head rotated to the side for a breath, but caught a lungful of water instead. She coughed and sputtered, unable to gather any oxygen as more water rolled down her throat. She had to surface. Treading water, she looked around and realized she was dangerously close to the back side of Haystack Rock. A storm was rolling in and the waves were swelling and pushing her toward the boulders.

She rotated and slanted her strokes toward shore. A huge wave lifted her in its trough and slammed her into the slimy rocks. Her head banged off the boulder before she plummeted underwater. Emmy held her breath, disoriented and dizzy. She kicked toward the surface but never broke through. Was she going up or down? She fought to be free of the water, her lungs burning, begging for oxygen.

Struggling in the murky ocean, she came to a realization—

if she just breathed in, she would drown. Then, she'd be with Grayson again and all the depression and fear of the past year would be gone. Everything moved slowly—the water, her body—but not her thoughts. She could be free. All she had to do was open up and inhale.

Her lips clamped shut, refusing to obey her idea. Her thoughts became more erratic and her vision darkened. She didn't really want to die. Her head was ready to explode. She was going to drown regardless. Maybe that was what her Father in Heaven wanted. Maybe it was time to be done and return to Grayson and her mom.

Suddenly, her head broke the surface, and she gasped for air. Choking, spitting, Emmy inhaled and her mind cleared. She beat at the water with her arms and legs to stay afloat. She was alive. There was a moment when she hadn't wanted to be, but now that she was, it was a glorious thing. She was going to be able to swim more. She was going to be able to teach her students and act in her plays. And maybe someday she could move passed the guilt and fear caused by Grayson's death and find happiness again. She said a silent prayer of gratitude.

Treading water as rain slashed down at her, Emmy looked around, unsure how far out she was, how long she'd been under, or if she had the strength to get back. Here she'd found the desire to live and now it might be taken from her.

She fought through mountainous waves and stinging rain. Thank heavens for her goggles or she would've been completely blind. Her muscles trembled. After just a short time her body was back to wondering if this fight was worth it or if she should just give up. She rolled onto her back and floated, trying to catch her breath and rest. A huge swell crested over her, filling her mouth with water. She attempted to tread water again but wave after wave beat at her, she could hardly catch her breath as salty liquid rushed in.

When drowning was almost a certainty, a strong arm hooked around her chest, flipped her over onto her back, and started tugging. Emmy didn't fight. She tried to kick to help her rescuer, but there was no strength left in her legs. Less than a minute later the man lifted her to her feet, and she was shocked to find footing. She spat out salt water, clung to him, and shouted over the howling wind, "I was that close?"

"I saw you struggling; you looked disoriented."

Emmy turned in the man's arms and about fell into the water again. "You!"

Not him.

Josh gave her a sad smile, his blue eyes as dark as the storm around them. "Would you prefer I let you drown?"

"I'd prefer you never touch me." She pulled from his grasp and stumbled, falling to her knees in the churning waves. Her feet and hands were numb from the cold, and she was so tired. She wanted to lie down and never move again.

He bent and lifted her into his arms. "Any other day I'd try to obey, but you need to get warm and let me check out that gash on your head."

Emmy struggled to be free of his iron clasp, but quickly realized it was futile. He was too strong, she was too weak, and the horrific thing was how good his solid chest felt. Leaning against him, she didn't allow herself to wrap her arms around his neck like she was tempted to do, but instead lifted her fingers and gently probed behind her ear. Blood trickled down her neck, and there was a watery red spot on his shirt. The salt in her hair suddenly stung the cut. She'd been too preoccupied with surviving and the rush of anger from seeing

32

him to realize she was bleeding.

He carried her like a small child up the beach and toward her house.

Emmy couldn't relax with the anger and attraction warring within her. Everyone claimed this man couldn't have hurt her husband. The police had never found the murderer. The investigation left no question that Josh was innocent. Not only had there been no evidence anywhere in his possession, several people had seen him a mile down the beach during the time of the murder.

But she had to have *someone* to blame, and the pull she felt toward Josh ticked her off enough that she focused all her anger on him. The rage didn't make her feel any better, but it did give her an excuse not to deal with the other feelings he aroused in her.

"How did you see me?" She studied the sharp angles of his face and remembered the dimples that had graced his cheeks when he'd smiled at her at the gym so long ago. Would she ever see his dimples again? Their interactions over the past year had not been pleasant for either of them.

He glanced down at her, his blue eyes compassionate and soft. He studied her for several seconds before admitting, "Sometimes I check on you."

"You *what?*"

His gaze never wavered as he continued slogging up the sandy beach. "I told you I'd do everything I could to help find the murderer. I'm still watching for him and watching out for you."

His admission should've terrified her, but for some reason it was endearing. She was terrified most of the time and the thought of him watching over her was...nice. But she couldn't admit that to him. "So the police claim you didn't kill my husband, and that gives you the right to appoint yourself my protector?"

He sighed. "Emmy."

She glowered at the familiar use of her nickname.

"Emmaline," he corrected. "I would protect you if you'd let me."

"Well, I don't need a protector. I'm doing just fine on my own."

"Yeah, I can see that." He stopped and pressed the outdoor shower button with his elbow, hurriedly rinsing their bodies of as much of the salt and sand as he could before carrying her up the stairs to her back patio. Emmy couldn't stop shivering. He set her on her feet and lifted the hair away from her wound.

Emmy should've moved out of his embrace, but her legs wobbled. She leaned against his broad shoulder. They were sheltered from the rain, but she was chilled clear through as the wetsuit held the cold water against her body.

"The cut isn't bad, but I can take you to the hospital if you'd like."

Her legs started to shake violently. "No. I'm fine. Thank you for helping me. I'll be fine."

Josh's eyebrows arched. "You can choose, I can take you to the hospital or I can take care of you here. But if you start showing signs of a concussion or need stitches, we're going in."

Emmy inhaled quickly at the thought of him taking care of her, of her allowing him into her house. It got her heart thumping a bit too fast, but if she could avoid the hospital, it would be worth it. "If you don't mind helping me here, I would appreciate it."

"I don't mind." He gently held her up with one arm, using the other hand to unzip her wetsuit.

Emmy pushed weakly at his chest with numb fingers. "You shouldn't undress me." Her chattering teeth distorted the words, but she could tell he got the meaning. His eyes widened as his face softened in a smile, and dang if those dimples didn't come out. Emmy was grateful for his arm supporting her as her legs went to goo.

"Under normal circumstances I wouldn't dare undress you."

"Why not?" Emmy demanded and then gasped. *Did I say that out loud?* Maybe she'd hit her head harder than she thought.

His smile got bigger. "Well, you usually snap like a turtle when you see me coming."

Emmy pressed her lips together, her skin tingling as he continued to work the zipper down and his fingers brushed her cold back. She couldn't help but notice his clean shaven face and the way his wet shirt clung to his impressive chest and shoulders. He was a beautiful man and he'd just called her a turtle. With her hair tangled, skin pale and blotchy, and her breath reeking of salt water, a turtle might be a step above what she looked like right now. "A turtle, now that's an attractive animal."

"I kinda like them."

"Just kinda?"

Josh laughed out loud. "Maybe if the turtle would stop snapping and let me get to know her it would be more than kinda."

Emmy's smile faded as she realized who she was flirting with. It didn't matter that he'd just saved her life. It didn't

35

matter that his touch and smile made her tremble. Though she knew the police were right and he hadn't hurt Grayson, this was the guy she'd had a semi-crush on when Grayson was still alive. It was just all wrong. Too wrong.

Josh set her on a patio chair and tugged the sleeves of her wetsuit down. His palms slid the length of her arms. Then he helped her stand and pulled the entire full-length suit over her hips and down her legs. She wasn't sure how he managed to touch so much of her body as he pulled the thick wetsuit off, revealing her one-piece Speedo swimsuit. She also wasn't sure how something that was wrong could feel this good. The pain in her head and the shivering almost disappeared as the rest of her body tingled from his touch and the way he shyly looked at her through his brown eyelashes.

He dropped the wetsuit on the patio, pulled off his dripping shirt, and swooped her into his arms again.

"You have got to stop doing that," Emmy said through rattling teeth, doing everything in her power not to look at his bare chest. Sadly, there was nothing she could do about his bulging muscles brushing against the skin of her arm, sending warmth through her chills.

Josh raised his eyebrows but didn't comment. At the locked door, he paused. She typed in the code and he swung it open then waited as she disabled the alarm system.

"Blankets and first aid supplies?" he asked.

"Upstairs." Emmy pointed. He carried her up the stairs and into her master bedroom. He set her on her feet but kept an arm around her waist. Pulling the blanket off her reading chair, he wrapped it around her and rubbed her hands, arms, and back through the blanket. Her extremities pricked with pain as the warmth returned.

36

"That better?" Josh asked.

She could only nod. All this physical contact was making her zing. The pull she felt toward him was more intense than ever. She glanced up. He was so close. His warm breath touched her forehead as she stared into those blue eyes. He smelled like salt water, and she wondered if he'd taste the same.

Josh's hands stilled on her back. He didn't try to pull her closer. He just studied her, the desire he felt evident in his gaze.

"Emmy?" he whispered. Asking permission. For what? To kiss her?

Emmy felt herself rising up to meet him as he leaned down. She almost nodded before shaking her head and hopefully knocking some sense in. The head shake caused the throbbing to start again. "Ouch." She pressed a hand to the back of her ear.

Josh took a deep breath and shook his own head, blinking a couple of times. "Do you have any saline?"

"In the bathroom."

He kept an arm on her back and helped her into the bathroom. Grabbing the saline from the medicine cabinet, he gently tilted her head over the sink and washed off the sand and blood behind her left ear. She winced at the pain.

"You don't need stitches." Josh patted it dry with a hand towel. The gentle movements should've been comforting, but with him looking at her like he couldn't stand to pull his eyes away, she was feeling anything but comfortable. She licked her lips and forced herself to meet his direct gaze.

"Are you warm enough?" he asked, his voice low and husky.

"Yes, thank you." But not all the warmth was from the blanket. Even with it wrapped around her shoulders, she was aware that her Speedo swimsuit didn't cover up as much skin as she'd like. She couldn't believe he was in her house. Part of her still wanted to kick him out, but she not only needed his help, she wanted it.

Josh helped her back to her bedroom and sat her in the overstuffed chair. He returned to the bathroom, coming back with tissue, a Band-aid, and Neosporin. Kneeling next to her polka-dotted chair, he blotted away the remaining blood, put Neosporin on the Band-aid, and then lifted her hair to press it into the right spot.

Emmy trembled. His tender movements made her doubt every suspicion she'd had. Was he some kind of gentle giant or just faking it to get her to trust him?

"I only needed one Band-aid?" From how bad her head throbbed, she assumed she'd been injured a lot worse than that.

"Yeah." He brushed the hair away from her face and neck, focusing on her eyes for a few seconds before dipping his head to look at the wound.

Emmy found herself holding her breath. His hands on her skin were heavenly. She'd hit her head repeatedly to have him touch her like that.

"Do you want me to take you to the hospital?" Josh asked. "You won't need stitches, but you might have a concussion from hitting your head on that rock."

Emmy was instantly dragged back to reality. "No, I hate that hospital." She'd begged the EMTs to take Grayson to the hospital though they were saying words like "DOA" and "Echo condition". She just couldn't have lived with herself if there'd been some kind of miracle the hospital could've performed.

She'd sat in the waiting room of the Providence Seaside Hospital for half an hour, praying and crying for a miracle before they told her he was gone. She'd known that the second she'd seen him stabbed in their basement, but she couldn't let herself believe it. The false hope as she'd waited and prayed had almost killed her. She knew she'd disillusioned herself, but vowed she'd never go back to that hospital.

"Well." Josh cleared his throat. "The other option is I stay here and watch over you."

Emmy gaped at him as he squatted next to her chair in his wet shorts. She couldn't help glancing over his chest and shoulders. *Oh, my.* "Um, no. Absolutely not. I'll call my neighbor. She'll come over and stay with me. I'm fine."

His eyes filled with sadness before he blinked and gave her a smile. "Okay. That sounds great. I'll bring you a phone."

Emmy only had to endure a few more minutes of looking at him and feeling his eyes on her before Kelton's mom, Abby, arrived. Emmy thanked Josh and then Abby directed him downstairs. Emmy closed her eyes, listening to Josh tell her friend what to watch for in case of a concussion and then say goodbye.

Abby pounded back up the stairs. With her hand over her generous bosom, she grinned at Emmy. "Now what did you do right in heaven to get rescued by that fine creature?"

Emmy closed her eyes and sighed. "I'm not sure if that one was a punishment or a reward."

Abby whistled, her dark braids bouncing happily. "I'd say definite reward. To see him in nothing but a pair of shorts? I'd go swim in that freezing ocean and hit my own head on a rock."

Emmy half-laughed, not willing to admit she'd probably do it all over again to spend more time alone with him. "I'm sure Tyrell would love to hear you talking like that."

Abby pushed a hand through the air. "Oh, he knows everyone in town has a huge crush on Captain Campbell. He'd just laugh at me. Now, what can I get you? Hungry? Thirsty? Ready for a bath? Some Tylenol? You sure you don't want to go to the hospital and have them check out your head?"

During the barrage of questions and answers, Emmy found herself thinking about Josh. He was so kind and competent. Guilt filled her as she realized she had no clue where he lived and though he was probably as cold as her, she hadn't offered him a towel or a blanket. Had he walked home in nothing but his shorts? The idea made her flush all over again.

Josh retrieved his sopping shirt from Emmaline's back porch and then went down to the beach to find his shoes. They were soaked. He picked them up, shoved his socks in, and started walking home in the driving rain.

For some reason, he was embarrassed. He'd saved Emmy's life. He should feel like some sort of hero, but instead, he kept thinking of how he shouldn't have taken every chance to touch her. Not that he'd touched anything he shouldn't, but just the feel of her skin was heaven.

He swallowed hard, remembering the pressure of her in his arms. She was almost impossible to resist, but he should've tried harder. At least he hadn't kissed her or taken any more advantage of the situation, which he also realized he easily could've done when she leaned up toward him. Did she feel the same pull of attraction he did? Most of the time he'd say no, but once in a while he wondered.

He walked through the rain-slicked streets the half mile inland to his small home. The driving rain pelted off his bare skin and chilled him further, but he allowed himself a small smile. At least he'd broken some of the barriers with her. The other times he'd seen her the past year, fire had shot from her eyes. When he reassured her that the police were working hard on her case or apologized for her misfortune, she'd snapped at him. He grinned. The turtle was not a bad analogy. But tonight he'd seen a softness in her, a vulnerability. Unfortunately, it just made her more attractive.

A car squealed down the road behind him with no headlights on, giving Josh little warning. It hurtled out of the dark and darted toward the sidewalk. Josh sprinted for the safety of a small porch. The black car dug through the wet grass, glancing off his hip and leg. Josh leapt onto the porch and the car fled onto the street and out of sight.

Josh limped back to the street to catch the license plate, but he moved too slowly and it was too dark. With the rain clouding his vision, the best he could do was guess at a make and model.

"Drunk drivers," he muttered, but something about the deliberate way they'd aimed at him made him wonder. He rubbed at his hip. Luckily the car had barely clipped him. He already felt the bruise swelling, but it could've been much worse.

No one came out of their houses or noticed his near miss. Four houses in a row had their lights off and one had a for sale sign in the front yard. Pricks of uneasiness added to the cold chilling his chest and arms. Josh hurried to his house, knowing he had nothing to report to the police but wanting to call one of his buddies on the force anyway. They'd been supportive of him throughout the investigation of Grayson's murder and Housley had become a close friend.

Josh walked in his back door and dropped all his wet clothes in the laundry room. After calling Housley and sharing his suspicions, he headed for the shower. His bungalow was nothing like Emmy's huge home, but it was clean, comfortable, and his.

Since moving to Cannon Beach, Josh had been flirted with and asked out by many of the women in town, but he only had eyes for the one woman who sometimes acted like she hated the sight of him.

Sadly, her grief and anger over her husband's murder seemed to be tied up with him. He hadn't been as in control of his feelings as he should've been tonight and hopefully that wouldn't hurt his chances even more, but he did feel like he was making progress. Maybe in another couple of years she'd actually want to be around him.

Chapter Seven

THE DAY WAS GRAY. The drizzly rain saturated Emmy's hair until the excess moisture dripped down her face. You'd think after two years of living in Oregon she'd learn not to leave the house without a raincoat.

She knelt next to Grayson's headstone, trailing her fingers over his name. The upright headstone was a beautiful white marble, shining through the darkness of the many storms. Emmy loved the personal touches on it—a laptop computer, a golf club, and a picture of him. She and his mom had designed it together, and thankfully his parents had understood why she wanted him buried here. Aunt Jalina had questioned the decision, of course, but this was their home and Emmy planned on growing old here and someday being laid to rest beside him. The convenience of visiting the reverent cemetery had been a healing balm.

The rain muted any outside noise and she stayed so long her linen pants were soaked. Often she would talk to Grayson, but today she didn't have much to say. She didn't want to tell him about almost drowning and Josh saving her. Would he be disappointed she hadn't joined him in Heaven last night? Grayson was the epitome of selflessness, but she still worried how he felt about her attraction to Josh. She sighed, wondering how that all worked. Maybe Grayson was so busy and happy up there he wasn't watching over her or listening to her every word.

A branch cracked behind her. Emmy turned in time to see a man in a hood disappear behind a tree. She watched for a minute, but he never materialized. A shiver ran through her that had nothing to do with the damp air.

Growing stiff from the wetness and lack of movement, she stood and then bent and pressed a kiss to her fingertips and onto the stone.

"Miss you."

As she walked away, she could've sworn someone watched her through the driving rain. She shivered and hurried to the relative safety of her Enclave.

Chapter Eight

EMMY KNOCKED ON THE THEATER owner's door. "James?"

"Come in, my dear."

She walked into the immaculate office, which boasted little more than a desk, a couple of hard chairs, and a gorgeous landscape portrait of the Italian countryside.

James gave her a smile, but his eyes were tired. They were in the last few days of performing *My Fair Lady*, and he still hadn't made a decision about their next play.

"Have a seat."

Emmy sat on the edge of her chair, clasping her hands together. She had several great ideas involving the theater that she wanted to talk to him about. They had collaborated on scripts and casting in the past. He had to like her new ideas.

"I want to bring some under-privileged children from Portland to perform with the group," she rushed out.

He tilted his head to the side. "Knowing you, it's all lined up and you've already assigned them parts in the next performance."

Emmy shrugged, hiding a grin. "I'll cover all their costs and they have a mentor who will be driving them and helping while they're here." She didn't explain the whole plan about feeding them dinner every night and sending snacks home for the hour drive. The organization she'd found helped children who were homeless or severely neglected, but hadn't yet been taken away by the state. She knew how it felt to be hungry and lonely. At least she'd had her mom some of the time.

"Sounds like a way for you to give back. I'll be happy to help."

"Thanks." Emmy paused for half a beat, but the next part of her plan was crucial to the children feeling part of the theater and being excited about it as well. "I hate to ask if you've decided on a script—"

James held up a hand. "Would you be interested in taking over the theater?"

Emmy straightened, blinking a couple of times. "Excuse me?"

"I'm exhausted. You could buy me out, or we could be partners, or you could take over and send a check to Florida when you make some money. Which I'm sure with your work ethic, talent, and imagination will not be a problem."

"Um." Dumbfounded, she didn't know what to say.

"I know, you didn't see this coming, but think about it for a moment, please. You'd do an amazing job and it would help."

He didn't need to explain. She knew exactly what he meant. It would help him retire and be able to take care of his wife who suffered from Multiple Sclerosis, but it would also help her to have a reason to get out of bed in the morning. She frowned. Was she ready to be this busy? To not be able to take it easy when the fearful, sleepless nights became too much? It sounded overwhelming, but she wanted this theater to be hers. She wanted it badly.

"I have no doubts you can be successful." He smiled wistfully. "I'll miss watching you perform when I move away."

Emmy didn't want to say goodbye to James, but running her own theater? James had asked for her input often, but she could now decide everything: casting, props, scripts, costumes. She barely withheld a squeal.

"Partners," she declared. "I'll buy into the theater. I need your expertise and this way you'll get a fat check now and dividends to live on."

The weariness in his eyes lifted a bit. "Partners it is. But..." His face wrinkled with a grin. "From Florida?"

"If you can help me through the summer season first."

He nodded. "Done."

She slid her chair closer to his desk, feeling as alive as she did when she swam and when Josh had held her in his arms the other night. "I'm thinking of *Beauty and the Beast.*"

James nodded. "It's bold. Can we afford the costumes?"

Emmy shrugged. Grayson had never told her about the million dollar life insurance policy and close to another million in various investments she was the beneficiary of. She could afford anything she wanted to afford. "I've still got some connections in L.A. We'll rent them. Think of little Madison playing Chip and Timothy will be an unbelievable Beast. The women will fall in love with his voice, his height will be imposing, and when he takes off his mask they'll swoon."

James arched an eyebrow. "Women usually do that when Timothy's around." He tapped his finger against his chin. "Who for Gaston?"

Emmy sat back for a minute then started laughing. "Kelton!"

James chuckled. "Overconfident and overly muscled. Perfect."

They discussed the casting and altering of the script until Emmy's stomach was eating its inner lining. As they said goodbye, Emmy knew she would miss her friend when he moved to Florida, but the opportunity to run this company was sunshine through a much too cloudy sky.

❦

Emmy released a deep breath of satisfaction. Her students made up the bulk of performers for the city's annual Fourth of July celebrations. They were all improving in skill and confidence. It was such a rewarding moment to share with their family and friends, making her almost feel like she had family.

Kelton finished with a blast of his deep bass, and she wished once again he'd take his talent more seriously. His voice was unreal. Perhaps a bigger role at the theater would spur him to work harder.

Kelton swept off the stage, hugged his mom, and then hurried to Emmy and lifted her off her feet. "How was that for ahhhh?"

"It was impressive, but if you don't stop hugging me, I'm going to get death threats from the entire female population of Seaside High." She winced at the words *death threats*.

Kelton didn't seem to notice. "I'd rather wait for you anyway." He grinned. A boy trapped in a man's body, but honestly one of her closest friends. He set her down and glanced over her shoulder. "Hey, it's Captain Campbell."

Emmy turned in the direction Kelton gazed. The oxygen fled from her lungs. She sidestepped out of Kelton's arms, jammed her toe on an exposed tree root, and would've fallen except *he* caught her. She should've forced herself to pull away, but Josh's touch was magical—warm, soothing, and exciting all at once. She fought to catch a full breath.

"Dude, I didn't know you and the captain...knew each other?" Kelton looked from one to the other.

Emmy finally pulled away, glancing at Kelton's disconcerted face. "I don't know him very well."

Josh gave her a hopeful smile. "I keep hoping she'll let me get to know her better."

Emmy's face flamed red, his nearness bringing back the memories of his tenderness after rescuing her. The wall she'd erected against him crumbled a bit more and she found herself wanting to get to know him better.

"Hey, Dude, I respect you and all that, but Emmy's waiting for me. Only five more years and I'll be through college."

Emmy laughed out loud. "I keep telling you I'm not attracted to younger men. Go flirt with someone your own age."

Kelton gave her a wounded look before saluting both of them and sauntering to a group of feminine admirers.

Josh chuckled. "Great kid."

"He's been such a good friend to me. Love that boy. Like a favorite nephew," she added quickly lest it sound like she *was* interested in younger men.

"So if you're not attracted to younger men, what type of guy are you attracted to?" The question was asked so quietly Emmy had to lean closer to hear over the noise of the carnival games and musical performances. He smelled like musk and salt water—two of her favorite scents.

She stiffened at his question. How was she supposed to respond? *I'm only attracted to you?* His nearness and smell almost overwhelmed her as she lied through her teeth, "I'm..."

49

She swallowed hard. "Not attracted to anyone."

Josh nodded and took a step back. "I understand. It's too soon."

Shame filled her. He'd been thinking of Grayson, but her thoughts were far from her husband. "Yes, um, thank you for understanding. If you'll excuse me, I'm missing my student's performance."

Josh gave her one more lingering glance before walking away. She watched him go, only turning back to the performance when the applause signaled it was done.

Chapter Nine

THE LACROSSE GAME WAS ALREADY STARTED when Emmy picked her way across the spongy turf to find Abby, Tyrell, and Kelton's brothers, Jerome and Tigre.

"Sorry I'm late," she explained when she drew closer. "I thought the game would be at the high school."

Abby waved a hand. "Football gets priority." She shooed Jerome out of a lawn chair at the end of their little family grouping. "Sit next to Captain Campbell."

Josh turned and smiled at Emmy from his lawn chair. "Josh," he corrected.

Emmy's heart stuttered. How had she not noticed him there? She tugged at the frayed edge of her cut-off jeans and hoped her ponytail was at least straight. She'd been cleaning her house when Kelton called to tell her he had an off-season game today and wanted her to come. She'd usually dress up a bit more, but she wanted to swim later and it was just an outside sporting event. But with Josh here, it suddenly changed to something else. She was supposed to sit by him?

Their section of lawn chairs exploded with screams and hoots, excited parents jumping to their feet. Emmy turned in time to see the red jerseys of Seaside High thumping each other on the back as the blue-jerseyed Banks' goalie hung his head and fished the ball out of the net. Emmy cheered along with everyone else, but when the cheering died and they all sat, she stayed standing, glancing sideways at Josh.

He smiled up at her and patted the arm of her chair in some sort of invitation. Emmy sighed and sank into the vinyl seat, not feeling the least bit comfortable.

"What number's Kelton?" she asked Jerome and Tigre who now shared a lawn chair. "Sorry I took your chair, you can have it back." Standing would help her keep some distance from Josh.

"Naw." Jerome waved her away. He pointed. "60."

Emmy looked down the field where Seaside's defense battled to stop Banks from scoring. She laughed that she'd asked. Kelton stood out with his height and ebony skin. Add that to the confident, aggressive way he moved, she would've recognized him anywhere. He batted another player's stick so hard it actually fell to the ground.

"Yard sale!" Jerome and Tigre screamed, jumping into the air in unison and celebrating.

"That's not nice," Abby admonished, though she had a grin on her face.

Kelton scooped the ball and passed it to the goalie, who sling-shotted it down the field. Since Kelton wasn't in the spotlight anymore, she found her attention wandering to the man seated at her side. He appeared to be watching the game, but she could feel him sneaking glances at her too. The air hummed with awareness.

One of the Seaside players got shoved out of bounds. He tossed the ball to the ref who gave it to the blue jerseys.

"What?" Emmy called out. "Come on Ref, he pushed him!"

"Totally legal," Jerome informed her.

"No way."

"Way."

Emmy reclined into her chair, embarrassed she'd yelled so loud.

Josh leaned over and touched her arm, the heat from his fingers pulsed through her bare skin. "I just yelled 'off sides' when one of the d-poles carried the ball to the offensive side of the field," he confided with a conspiratorial smile.

"Also totally legit as long as a middie stays back," Tigre said.

Emmy appreciated Josh trying to make her feel better, but wasn't happy when he removed his hand. "What is a d-pole?"

"A defender, like Kelton. They have the longer poles."

"Yeah," Tigre said, "But we also have a long-pole middie."

"Wow. I am confused."

Josh smiled at her. "Stick close to me and I'll try to explain."

Emmy's entire body warmed from his smile and the thought of sticking close to him.

Jerome leaned across her. "You play lax, dude?"

"I wish." Josh gestured at the field. "They didn't have this at my school so I had to play football."

Jerome's face pinched. "Bummer for you. Lax rules."

"I can see that," Josh said.

Emmy hid a smile. She refocused on the field in time to see Kelton bearing down on a much smaller blue jersey. He knocked the kid to the ground then scooped up the ball, ran to the center of the field, and passed it off. Kelton ran back to his position and offered the other player a hand up. The poor kid shook as he got to his feet but fist-bumped Kelton, so she figured there were no hard feelings.

"And that wasn't a foul?" she asked the twins.

"Penalty," Tigre corrected. "No way. He had his hands together, didn't extend his elbows, and was in the front. My bro is boss at legal hits."

Emmy laughed. "I can imagine. Do you play defense too?"

"I'm a middie."

"I'm an attack and Dad's coach for the junior league," Jerome said. "We keep telling Mom we need one more bro to play goalie then we're set."

Abby rolled her eyes. "And I keep telling them they did me in and they're lucky to have the bros they have."

Tyrell's large hand closed around Abby's. "We could at least try for one more boy."

Abby yanked her hand back. "I am done. You and your next wife can have fun."

Tyrell's deep chuckle rolled across them. "Think I'll keep the beautiful wife I have."

"I think that's a good choice."

Tyrell grabbed her hand again and she let him tug her closer for a lingering kiss.

"They're kind of gross," Jerome whispered to Emmy.

"They're cute. You're lucky." Emmy was surprised when her throat caught and she couldn't say anymore. When she was a child, she would have given anything for an intact family. Actually, it would be pretty great even now.

"I guess." Jerome made a face and turned away.

Josh was looking at her again. "Great family."

Emmy nodded. She stared at the field so she didn't have

to hold his gaze. A blue-jersey sprinted toward the goal. He'd steered clear of Kelton, but had underestimated Kelton's speed. As the kid raised his stick to score, Kelton came from the side and poked the bottom of the stick. The ball popped out and Kelton scooped it out of the air.

"Wow. He's impressive," Emmy muttered.

"Beastly," Jerome corrected.

Emmy shared a glance with Josh, smiling.

"Middie back!" a Seaside player yelled, jabbing his stick in the air.

"That's so Kelton can cross the midfield line as a d-pole," Tigre explained.

Kelton was almost to the other end of the field, holding his long pole aloft, when a Banks' player came at him, but Kelton dodged and kept sprinting toward the goal.

Emmy jumped to her feet with the rest of the family. "He's going to score," she whispered.

Kelton dove and shot at the net. A defender from the other team whacked him in the back of the neck. Kelton flattened to the ground. The shot went in but the screams of triumph were short-lived when everyone realized Kelton wasn't moving.

Emmy didn't stop to think as she sprinted across the field, shouting, "Kelton!"

She knelt by his side, the other lacrosse players moving out of her way. "Kelton?" He stayed face down, not moving.

The coaches and Josh were suddenly there. Josh knelt next to Emmy and pressed his fingers to Kelton's neck. "Strong pulse," he reported. He gently probed Kelton's spine then looked up at the coaches. "I don't feel anything but I don't want to move him."

Kelton groaned and slowly rolled over onto his side.

The players let out a collective sigh of relief. Emmy noticed Abby creeping along the sidelines. As soon as she saw Kelton moving, she drew back. What? Abby was hyper protective of her boys. Why wasn't she pushing Emmy out of the way?

Kelton squinted, focusing in on her. "Emmy?" He croaked. "What are you *doing?*"

She patted his shoulder. "I think you got knocked out. I was worried when he hit you." She straightened and glanced at the boy in blue who had hit him, kneeling a short distance away. "You had better never do that again. I hope they eject you from the game or something."

The boy blinked at her.

"Emmy," Kelton whispered.

She leaned down. "What do you need, sweetie? We'll get you to the hospital. You're going to be fine."

"You're making me look wussy in front of my lax bros."

Emmy straightened and glanced around. All of the players, coaches, and fans stared at her like she had two heads. "Oh." She brushed a stray hair back into her ponytail. "So, you're okay?"

Kelton pushed his way to his feet; everyone stood back, and the fans cheered. "Course I'm okay." He winked at her before picking up his stick.

Josh stepped forward. "Kelton, I'm going to have to insist that you go get checked out."

"Dude." Kelton groaned. "I thought you were chill."

"Not about this. You could have a concussion or neck injury."

The coaches agreed and ushered Kelton to the players' sidelines where Abby and Tyrell waited. Josh followed Emmy back to the other sideline where the fans gawked. He put a strong hand on her back as if to support her through the unfriendly wall. She turned to him. "Why is everyone staring at me?"

"Because you're so pretty."

She smiled at him but knew he was trying to make her feel less awkward.

They reached Tigre and Jerome. "Did you *seriously* just do that?" Jerome asked.

"What?"

"You don't run out on the field when a lax bro gets hurt. It's like, in the rules."

Emmy's mouth dropped open. "You're kidding me. Kelton could've been killed and I'm supposed to sit here?"

"Well, duh. Didn't you see Mom? She moved as close as she could get, but she never, ever goes on the field. We'd disown her."

"That is the stupidest thing I've ever heard!"

Tigre lifted one shoulder. "We didn't write the rules, we just live by them."

Emmy turned to Josh. "Is he kidding me right now?"

Josh shook his head. "If a mom or girlfriend goes on the field it's generally looked down upon."

"That is insane."

"Yeah, I agree."

Jerome glared at them. "Captain, you can't be siding with the girl. They'll think they have to baby us all the time. Dad explained it to Mom when Kelton first started lax. Moms can love on us all the time except for on the field, then we gotta be tough."

Emmy shook her head, but was starting to understand this ridiculous philosophy. This was their field of battle, their chance to prove themselves as men, and they didn't want sympathy when they were injured.

"If I got hurt on the field, you could come running," Josh whispered in her ear.

Emmy turned to him. He was so close she could feel his warm breath on her cheek. "I hope you never get hurt anywhere."

He smiled and she had to resist touching one of his shallow dimples.

"Emmy." Abby ran up to them. "Can you take the boys home? We're going to the hospital."

"Sure. Is he okay?"

She twisted her fingers together. "I think so. But I want to get him checked out anyway. Thank you, Josh, for insisting he get help. He usually just keeps playing, but he respects you so he listened."

Josh nodded. "Let me know what they find out."

"We will." She turned to her younger boys. "You two go home and be good."

"Can we watch the rest of the game?"

"That's up to Emmy." Abby thanked her and ran to where Tyrell and Kelton were slowly making their way to the parking lot. Kelton didn't want to claim he was hurt, but he looked beat.

"How about it?" Tigre asked.

"Oh, we definitely need to stay," Emmy said. "You need to teach me more about lacrosse."

The twins and Josh all smiled at her. Emmy settled back into her chair, grateful Kelton was going to get help and really excited to spend a bit more time with Captain Campbell.

Chapter Ten

EMMY USUALLY ONLY VISITED THE GRAVE every few weeks, but she was so excited about the prospect of running her own theater she wanted to share it with her husband. Grayson would've encouraged her and loved seeing her become a businesswoman. She thought about Josh and wondered what he would think of the idea, but quickly dismissed the thought. She hardly knew him.

It was raining again, but that didn't deter her as she spilled every thought—from the theater changes to running out on the lacrosse field. Grayson would've laughed and probably been as gentle and understanding as Josh had been. She sighed; there she went thinking of Josh again.

"I'd better go. I've got practice for *My Fair Lady* in an hour." She traced the picture of him with her finger. "You would've loved this one. Timothy does such a great job as the professor. I really struggled with that Cockney accent, but I think I'm doing okay now." She smiled sadly. "You always said I could do any accent. That's the only reason I kept working so hard instead of begging James to switch scripts." She laughed at her own joke. They both knew James would never switch a script once the play was in motion.

The air was eerily quiet as her soft laugh dropped into

the void. She sobered and pressed her fingertips to her mouth and then to his picture. Her fingers brushed his nose instead of his lips and she had to redo the gesture. It made her want to cry, but she'd done enough crying the last year.

As she straightened and stiffly walked away, she saw a tall figure lean around a large pine tree. Her mind flashed back to a few days ago when a man in a hood seemed to be watching her. She rubbed her hands along the sleeves of her jacket.

She couldn't see the person's face, but the way he angled toward her made her feel like a rabbit in the cross hairs. Turning toward her car, she walked quickly away. The hair on the back of her neck stood on end. Walking just wasn't enough to ease her worries. She broke into a run. Movement came behind her, but she didn't look back, focusing all her energy on getting away.

She slipped on the grass, crying out more from fear than pain when her knee hit the wet ground. She jumped back up and was only a few feet from the car when she dared to check if that man was really chasing her or if she was going crazy. He wasn't far behind and moved quickly. His hood blew back, revealing a face covered with a grotesque Halloween-type mask. Emmy screamed, grabbed the door handle, and flung herself into her Enclave. She slammed the door, hit the lock button, and quickly twisted the key in the ignition.

Her tires squealed out of the cemetery. She looked desperately for the man, praying he wasn't pursuing. Her heart thudded uncontrollably. She kept checking her rearview mirror, but eventually her pulse slowed down as she convinced herself he wasn't coming after her. It was just hard to admit the truth. He had disappeared.

Chapter Eleven

EMMY PEEKED THROUGH OF THE SIDE of the heavy velvet curtain. The lights in the house were still on. She had plenty of time. Her eyes swept the people filtering in and settling into the worn fabric seats. It only took a few seconds to spot his longish blond hair and broad shoulders. He glanced at the program, not noticing her scrutiny. It looked like he was alone.

She sighed happily, hugging herself in her ratty costume. Josh was here. This was the last performance of My Fair Lady, and she'd hoped he would come. She didn't allow herself to think about why it was so important, but quickly said a prayer of gratitude. She hadn't been nervous before, but now her stomach swam.

"Who are you looking for?" a gravelly voice spoke near her ear, bristly hair brushing her cheek.

Emmy let out an involuntary scream and jumped. She turned, surprised to see Shane standing much too close. She took a step back but stopped when she hit the curtain. It wouldn't do for her to fall onto the stage. There was no reason for her to be afraid, it was just Shane, but seeing that guy at the cemetery the other day had really pushed her anxiety over the edge.

She shook her head. "No one, it's just fun to feel the excitement from the audience before a performance."

He nodded, smiling shyly down at her. "You're the best actress and singer I've ever heard."

"Well, thank you, Shane." Emmy returned his smile. He was usually so shy around her he could barely speak. She needed to help him feel comfortable. He did an amazing job with the props and background; prop manager was definitely not a position she wanted to worry about replacing when James left.

He licked his lips and glanced at the curtain as he spoke. "Do you think, um, maybe sometime, you and I could go get a bite to eat after rehearsal one night?"

Emmy kept the smile on her face, not sure how to let this gentle man down carefully. He was kind, but definitely not what she was looking for. Josh's image flashed through her mind. It would be hard for anyone to compete with him. Yet she couldn't risk offending Shane when it was being announced tonight that she was taking over the theater.

"Are you ready, Miss Doolittle?" Timothy swept close to her and offered his elbow, looking every inch the handsome gentleman in a vest, suit, and top hat.

Emmy laughed, relieved to be swept from this predicament. "Yes, Professor." She grasped onto his arm, trying not to notice Shane's downcast face. "Goodbye, Shane, we'll see you at the party." She didn't want to give him false hope, but she couldn't just walk away without saying anything.

Shane lit up. "Sounds good."

Timothy leaned in as they walked. "You need to discourage him. Have you seen how he watches you?"

"No." She was always in her own world when acting, but she should've noticed if he paid her extra attention off stage.

"He's got it bad for you, and it doesn't help that you're single now." Timothy winced. "Sorry, Em. You're just so oblivious to the way men look at you. Like you assume they only appreciate your artistic ability." He shook his head. "I've tried to watch out for you, especially with Grayson gone."

Emmy searched his face, hoping it was her imagination that he looked hopeful. She loved Timothy as a friend, but it could never be anything more. "I really appreciate you being there and not being one who looks or asks me out."

Timothy swallowed and then smiled wistfully. "Wish I could say different, but you're like a little sister to me." His eyes darkened but then regained their characteristic twinkle. "Of all the rotten luck."

"And you're like a brother to me. Plus, I wouldn't want to compete with all your female fans."

Timothy grinned. "What's a guy to do?"

"It must be hard."

He winked.

They moved into position and Emmy knew she needed more friends like Timothy, not men who wanted to take her on a date. She just wasn't ready. She thought of Josh sitting in the audience. Okay, maybe she wanted one man to look, desire, and take her on dates.

The performance pulled Emmy into another world as she became Eliza Doolittle. She knew personally how hard it was to be poor and downtrodden and then to rise to your full potential. As Eliza, the professor both inspired and infuriated her. Falling in love with him and having that love returned were not in her plans but couldn't be helped.

All too soon they took their bows and hurried to greet the crowd after the curtain closed. Though she'd given her whole heart to this performance, it had been in the back of her mind all night that Josh was out there, watching her. It added a level of intimacy and excitement to everything.

She greeted all the fans who filtered passed, wondering where he was as the crowd trickled down. She almost went up on tiptoes to search for him, but refrained. Had he left early? The bitter taste of disappointment obliterated the thrill she'd been experiencing. Maybe he hadn't enjoyed the performance and didn't want to face her. He might have been called away for an emergency; he or someone else could be in danger. She forced herself to keep smiling at the people who were gushing over her talent and telling her the theater would be nothing without her and her handsome co-star.

Josh appeared at the very end of the line, a shy grin showing off his dimples and a beautiful spring bouquet in his hands. Her heart paused for a moment, then beat at triple speed.

Timothy was still close by her side, his costume smelling stale and sweaty from multiple nights of wear under the bright lights without a dry cleaning opportunity. He moved a bit closer. The spicy cologne he always wore to override the costume stench made her nose twitch.

"He's okay," Emmy whispered out of the side of her mouth.

One of the college students interning from Portland moved in on Timothy's right and babbled about his talent. He cast a glance back at Emmy, but she was having a hard time focusing on anything but Josh's smile.

Josh offered her the flowers. "You were amazing. I can

honestly say I've never really enjoyed *My Fair Lady* until tonight."

Emmy shivered at the feel of his warm fingers touching hers as she took the bouquet and smiled. "Thank you. I'm glad you came."

"So am I." He stood there, his blue eyes admiring her, and his dimples on fine display.

Emmy was in her own little world smiling back at him until Timothy cleared his throat. The girl with him suddenly fell silent. Emmy glanced around and noticed there were no other patrons in the building, and the entire cast and crew were watching them. "Oh, um. It was great to see you, but I probably should..."

"I could, wait, maybe we could go to Mo's and get a shake."

Emmy didn't even like Mo's, but she'd never wanted a shake so badly in her life.

Timothy pushed against her arm. "The party."

"Oh." She exhaled. "I'm sorry. We have a cast party. Closing night and all."

"Okay." He raked a hand through his hair. "Maybe some other time."

"Definitely." She was as happy with her impulsive response as he seemed to be.

He gave her one more grin before striding out into the night. Emmy watched him go. Timothy pumped his eyebrows. "Maybe there's one man who you don't think of as a brother."

"No brotherly feelings at all for that man," Emmy admitted as she kicked herself for not inviting Josh to come back for her after the party.

Timothy stayed close by her side throughout the evening,

making it easy to avoid any alone time with Shane. Emmy dreaded responding to his request for a date.

Everyone cheered when James announced Emmy would be taking over the theater, then groaned when James admitted he was retiring to Florida. The entire night was just about perfect. If only she would've agreed to meet Josh after.

Chapter Twelve

JOSH'S HEART THUMPED SO LOUD it made his head pound. Sweat poured down his back from his turnout coat. He raced toward the burning house, his partner, Axel, at his side. The crew behind them still hadn't punched into the water supply and the people trapped in the house didn't have time to wait. He slammed his ax into the door and jumped out of the way. The fire and smoke didn't disappoint, billowing out to grab more oxygen before swooshing back in.

Josh took some deep breaths from his air tank before motioning to Axel that he'd go first. He charged through the door. The flames licked his coat and devoured the furniture around him. Sweat trickled into his eyes. He blinked but couldn't clear the stinging completely. He searched for any sign of life in the front room while Axel pushed through to the kitchen. Over the roar of the fire he listened for something human and thought he heard a faint cry.

He rushed in the direction of the cries, coming to a closed door at the end of a short hall. The door opened easily. Smoke layered the room but thankfully no fire yet. He hollered to Axel before shutting the door to keep more smoke out. A young couple cowered on the floor next to a sleigh bed. The woman clutched a toddler who screamed uncontrollably.

Josh bobbed his head to them, yelling, "We'll get you out of here." Though he doubted they heard or understood a word.

He glanced for an escape route. He couldn't take them through the house without protective gear. The window was the only option. It was broken and the screen gone but the decorative metal bars made it impossible to get through. Josh fumbled with the safety lever for a few seconds, awkward with his gloves, before realizing it was broken. He slammed the butt of his ax into it several times and pushed. Nothing.

Blinking away the salt in his eyes, he glanced out at the backyard, wishing the rapid intervention team would get here. Smoke poured under the door and the temperature in the room was unbearable. He gave the family a reassuring nod, though he felt more panicked than he had in a long time. Where was Axel?

Turning the ax around, he heaved it over his head and used every ounce of strength to smash the blade into the release mechanism. Sparks and bits of the shattered lever flew. Josh swung at it several more times, each hit damaging the lever more. He dropped the ax and pushed at the metal bars. They didn't give. *Oh, no.* Had he made it worse by banging on it?

He braced his legs against the bed and shoved with everything he had. The bars groaned open. He said a silent prayer of gratitude and motioned for the family. They were already on their feet and ready to escape. Josh assisted the wife through first, handing her the little one. The husband nodded and coughed his gratitude before leaping after his wife.

Josh breathed a sigh of relief and then turned to see the door still closed behind him. Axel was in trouble.

❧

Emmy drove home from the theater, leaning her head back against the headrest. It was a great kind of exhaustion. They'd started rehearsals for *Beauty and the Beast* a few days after the last performance of *My Fair Lady.* Some of the cast would've liked a break, but it was summertime and they needed to have another play going for their busiest season. So far she couldn't have asked for better practices. The children from Portland were delightful, and Kelton and Timothy made the entire production a lot of fun. She was happier than she'd been in a long time.

Red lights strobed against the houses in the neighborhood she usually cut through to go home. Smoke billowed into the air above the roofline. She veered to go around, but suddenly thought of Josh. What if he was dealing with the fire?

Her breath caught in her throat at the thought of him in danger. She shook her head. She shouldn't care so much; she barely knew the man. But she pulled to the curb a few houses down from the controlled chaos. She walked quickly to the back of the crowd, trying to peek over shoulders and see what was going on. Even this far away she could feel the heat from the fire.

Paramedics swarmed a young family wearing oxygen masks. The wife sobbed and clung to her toddler. The husband reached through the EMTs to pat his wife on the arm. Emmy exhaled. It appeared the home's occupants had been rescued. The firemen were spraying the neighboring houses and the large trees in the yard, but not directly onto the house where smoke and fire poured through windows.

Weird. She looked around for Josh but didn't see him. The other fireman's faces were somber. Shouldn't they be happier that the family was safe?

"That house is coming down," one of them yelled at another. "We need to go defensive."

"Not until Campbell and Axelrod are cleared."

"I'm going in," a third man yelled, pulling his face mask on.

All the breath rushed from Emmy's body. "No," she cried out, not realizing she'd spoken aloud. The trusses swayed, one stiff shove and the roof would collapse. The sheeting had already buckled in several places leaving gaping holes.

A tall, dark head turned in the crowd, looking straight at her. "Emmy?" Kelton gestured and she made her way to his side nearer the front of the onlookers.

"Josh is in there?" Emmy asked.

"That's the word. He rescued that family and the dad thought he would follow them out. He must've gone back for his partner." He gestured to one of the other firemen. "And the Chief won't let anyone go in after them." He pounded on his chest. "Give me a suit. I'll save the Captain."

"No." Emmy grabbed his arm, not wanting anyone else she cared about to be in harm's way. Cared about? Is that what she was feeling for Josh? She couldn't stand the thought of him suffering in that fire. Tears leaked down her cheeks just thinking about it. She started to pray quietly. "Please bring him out alive. Please."

A side window suddenly shattered, glass spraying the lawn. Emmy gasped. The fire was exploding windows. How could Josh possibly survive? A fireman sagged against the window frame. He flopped headfirst onto the grass.

The other firemen doused him with water, then lifted

him from the ground and carried him to the ambulance. They pulled his head gear off, revealing tight black curls. Not Josh.

Where was he? Emmy wrung her hands together, praying, not knowing what she'd do if he didn't appear.

The air conditioning unit teetered and then plunged through the roof, causing a terrific bang and more smoke and flames to shoot up.

Hands appeared on the window frame then a head. The firefighter slowly climbed through and walked away from the house. They doused him with water, knocking him back a foot but he regained his stance. He disconnected his air hose, then lifted his helmet and hood, revealing Josh's handsome face and blondish-brown hair wet with sweat.

Emmy cheered along with the rest of the crowd, yelling a little louder than everyone else, but this was a reason to celebrate.

"Whoa, Emmy." Kelton grinned. "Bit excited?"

"Just glad he's okay." She couldn't help edging to the front of the crowd, aching to hear his voice, wanting to push through the police caution tape and go to him. He told her at the lacrosse game that she could go to him if he got hurt, but she wondered if he'd just been trying to make her feel better. This was his field of battle and she didn't want to undermine him like she had Kelton.

Josh didn't seem to notice anyone but the police and firemen crowding in to hear what happened and the EMTs ready to administer first aid. The entire crowd quieted, listening in on his conversation, restless for news as well.

"Pinned under a ceiling beam," Josh panted for air as he talked to another fireman. Steam poured from his suit and skin. "Miracle I lifted it off of him and somehow got to the window. Got really disoriented."

"Someone's been praying you safe," the other man said.

"Yeah." Josh nodded and then looked directly at her. His blue eyes widened. "Emmy." Her name came out like a reverent whisper.

She smiled and gave him a stupid little wave. "I'm so glad you're okay."

"Thanks." He returned her smile with a tired one of his own before he was surrounded again and ushered to the ambulance.

"What was that?" Kelton arched an eyebrow.

"He's been a...a friend to me."

"Just a friend?" Kelton chuckled, but didn't make her answer. "He's cool. I'm glad you figured it out. For a while you didn't like him much."

"No," she admitted, reddening at the thought of how rude she'd been to him this past year.

"The dude is beastly. Saved a couple of us once when we were making acetylene bombs. He's chill, didn't get all preachy on us."

Emmy felt her heart melt a little more. Kelton thought of Josh as beastly, but to Emmy he was a hero and so much more.

Chapter Thirteen

EMMY HATED NIGHTTIME.

Once her morning alarm went off, her day was pretty full. She woke early each day to exercise, would hold lessons all morning, practiced singing or her parts at home or went for a swim in the afternoon, and then went to rehearsals in the evenings. The only time she was truly alone was at night. Before the notes and Grayson's murder she'd often forget to lock the doors at night. Now when she came home she made sure every blind or curtain was closed, every deadbolt secured, and the alarm system armed. She used to enjoy reading before going to bed, but she now read with her cell phone in one hand, fidgeting at every sound and imagining frightening knife-wielding men. Eventually, her eyes would droop shut and she would be lost in sleep for a few short hours.

At least it wasn't Josh she imagined with a knife anymore. She smiled to herself. The little bit she was learning about Captain Campbell she liked. She liked a lot.

She sat on the couch, trying to read until she was sleepy enough to brave going to bed. A soft tapping came from the back patio as if someone was walking across it. Ice rubbed along Emmy's spine. Instantly, her heart beat so fast she had to pant for breath. Was it the murderer? The man with the mask at the cemetery?

She wanted to hide behind the sofa and call the police, but she wouldn't overreact. It could be a tourist; they'd invaded her porch before. She forced wobbly legs to support her and tiptoed across the rug. Her cell phone dug into her palm. At the sliding glass door she flipped off the lights in the living room and switched on all the exterior lights. She jerked back the curtain, proud of herself, though she trembled violently.

A tall man jumped from the patio stairs to the sand and darted across the beach. His large rain jacket billowed out as he ran, hiding his shape. A baseball cap shadowed his features.

Emmy's entire body shuddered. She watched through the glass until she was certain the person was gone, feeling as if her stare was the only thing keeping him running. If she lost focus, he'd come back. She quickly dialed 911. The operator assured her they'd send someone right over.

The doorbell rang. Emmy jumped. The police couldn't be that quick. She checked the lock on the back door, pulled the curtain tight, and flipped the inside lights back on. She gripped her cell phone as she hurried to the nine-foot wooden door and peeped through the sidelight. Josh shifted from one foot to another with flowers in hand. Relief washed over her. She turned the deadbolt and ripped the door open, grinning at him.

He returned the smile with a beautiful one of his own. Her heart thumped. Anxious to bring the safety he represented into the house and shut the door on all the horrible things in the dark, she stepped back and said, "Come in." The mixture of comfort and excitement she felt with him here helped calm her anxiousness, until the high-pitched wail of her alarm cut through the night.

"Oh, crap." She ran to the wall to type in the code. The alarm silenced but her cell phone rang immediately. "Sorry," she mouthed to Josh as she reassured the security company that she'd just forgotten to disable the alarm.

Josh shut the door behind him. Emmy hung up the phone and set it on the entry table. "Sorry," she said again. "I don't get many visitors."

"It's okay. Do you like the alarm system?"

"Not really, but after…" Judging from the look on his face she didn't need to finish.

He exhaled slowly, clutching the flowers.

It hit Emmy how trusting she was being. All the safety she'd felt moments earlier started to waver. "You, um, weren't on my back patio in a raincoat and hat earlier?"

Josh's eyebrows arched, complete surprise written in his eyes. Relief swept over her. How she knew she could trust him now when she hadn't before was a mystery, but she did, and that trust brought a sense of comfort she hadn't had since before Grayson died.

"No." He stared at her. "Someone was?"

"Yes, but he ran away when I turned on the lights. Sorry I asked, I don't think you'd go creeping on back patios."

"No, I wouldn't but…" He shook his head. "The day your husband was murdered I saw a tall guy wearing a raincoat and hat watching your house."

Her mouth fell open, questions filling her mind.

"How long ago did you see the guy on the patio?" he asked.

"Right before you came."

"I'll be back." He pressed the flowers into her hands, turning toward the door. "Wait, do you have a flashlight?"

"Sure." Emmy rushed into her kitchen, found a flashlight and returned, handing it to him. "What are you going to do?"

"Follow his footprints." Josh sprinted off her front porch and around the side of the house.

"Wait," Emmy called, but he was already gone.

Emmy closed the door, turned the deadbolt, and leaned against it. Her heart pounded. Would Josh find the guy? Could it possibly be the man who murdered Grayson? She would give anything for some closure and the chance to live a worry-free life again. She didn't move as the possibilities of true freedom grew in her mind. But then the worry filtered in. What if it was the murderer and he hurt Josh? Should she go out there and try to help? Warn Josh to watch for knives?

As she debated what to do, the door pounded against her back. Emmy leaped into the air. She peeked through the sidelight. Josh. She turned the deadbolt, swung the door open, and gestured him inside. "Did you find him?"

He shook his head. "He was smart. I followed the footprints down to the water. I searched but couldn't see a match leaving the water. I talked to Housley. He's bringing a dog to sniff out the guy's smell from your patio and see if he can pick up a scent." He shrugged. "Will be tough though if he stayed in the water long."

Emmy sighed. "Thanks for trying. It was probably just some tourist trying to look in my windows."

Josh nodded. "Maybe, but we keep hoping for a break in your case."

Her case. Emmy shook her head, dispelling the awful memories. "Thank you for the flowers."

His blue eyes lit up. "I wanted to congratulate you.

Kelton told me you took over the play house and started rehearsals for *Beauty and the Beast*."

Emmy inhaled the wonderful smell of the lilies, begonias, roses, and daisies clasped in her hand. "Thank you. I'm really excited about it."

"You'll make the prettiest Belle ever." His face colored.

Emmy had never been so flattered. "It's a fun role."

They stood there for half a second, awkward and staring at each other.

"Would you like to come sit down?"

"Can I take you to dinner tomorrow?"

They both spoke at the same time, rushing out their sentences as if someone were going to slap a hand over their mouths.

Emmy laughed. "I would love to go dinner."

Josh grinned. "I would love to come sit down."

She turned and walked through the entry into the open kitchen, dining, and living room area. He followed. She couldn't help but wonder what he thought of her house. Was it as ridiculously big as it seemed to her right now? She'd thought a hundred times about selling it and getting away from the memories of Grayson's death, but selling it meant losing the memories of their brief marriage.

"Have a seat." She gestured to the living room and hurriedly found a vase, filled it with water, and plunged the flowers in. His eyes followed her, and she had a hard time doing the simple task.

"Your home is beautiful," he said.

"Thanks." Wiping her hands on a dishtowel, she found her gaze drawn to his as she walked across the bumpy hardwood floor to the plush living room rug. Panic fluttered in her chest. Where should she sit? He was on the sofa. She could sit next to him without getting too close. No, that would be pushing it. She opted for one of the overstuffed chairs. "Were you injured in the fire the other night?"

Josh shook his head. "No, but Axel busted his leg and had to be treated for smoke inhalation."

"I'm sorry. That was so heroic of you to save him." Great. She sounded like a Josh-groupie.

"Thanks." Josh focused completely on her. She felt the pull that always happened when he really looked at her. She wanted to leave the chair and snuggle up to him on the sofa. Wrapping her hands around the chair cushion, she held on for stability.

"Does the alarm system help you feel safe?" he asked.

Emmy gulped, pulled back to reality. "As safe as I can with the murderer still out there somewhere."

"The notes have stopped." It wasn't a question; he obviously was in contact with the police department.

She bobbed her head.

"We're going to find the guy, Emmy." He reached across and patted her knee. It should have reassured her. Instead, she felt the jumble of trembling attraction like some silly teenager.

"I hope so." She sighed. "I thought maybe the police were right and the guy wasn't from around here. It's been a year and there haven't been any notes or anything." She paused. "Well, except for that guy tonight and I saw some weird guy at the cemetery a few days ago."

He leaned closer. "Did he look the same?"

She searched her memory but couldn't see passed the fear and finally shrugged. "They were both tall."

Josh looked pensive for a minute. "He's going to make a mistake, and we're going to find him. You need the closure."

Emmy nodded. Closure sounded wonderful. "I definitely don't want someone like that on the loose. It's so terrifying that he might still be out there watching me or be someone I see every day at the grocery store or the gym." Her face filled with warmth. "I mean. Well, I didn't *mean*."

Josh didn't look away.

Emmy had to tell him. "I know you didn't kill him."

He exhaled and gave her a soft smile. "It means a lot to hear you say that."

"I'm sorry I blamed you."

"No. Don't apologize. It just makes me sick that you went through that and still have to worry."

His blue eyes were so warm. Emmy was glad she'd forgiven him. Now she was more than ready to change the subject. "You obviously didn't stop going to the gym." She pointed at the thick bicep and triceps muscles poking out of his T-shirt. The sight of those brawny arms made her a bit weak. "Why did you change times?"

"At first I did it so you wouldn't have to see me."

She winced. "Thank you. I feel bad, but I really hated you for a while."

"I noticed." He splayed his hands. "But you don't hate me now?"

"Not even close." She let out a giggle a ten-year old would be proud of, and he rewarded her with a smile that showed his dimples. *Oh, my.* She kept talking so she didn't do something she might regret. "Why don't you come to the gym early anymore?"

"It's crazy to wake up at five a.m. when I could go at six-thirty and still fit in a good workout and breakfast before my shift."

"I'm one of the crazies. I like the morning, plus during the school year my students come pretty early."

"I love that you're still teaching."

He glanced at her state-of-the-art kitchen filled with granite counters, top-of-the-line stainless steel appliances, and gorgeous cherry cabinets. Emmy hoped he wasn't thinking about the fact that she had been a suspect for a while because of all the money Grayson left solely to her. The investigator had finally stopped pursuing that angle when there was no proof and witness after witness, most of them Grayson's family, insisted Emmy would never do such a thing.

"My students are amazing. I'd lose a part of me if I stopped teaching them."

"I hear all the time how amazing you are."

"Thanks." She blushed from his compliment and the sincerity of his gaze.

He stood. "I'd better go and let you get some rest."

Emmy stood with him, wishing he'd stay and wishing she really would fall asleep when he did go. After seeing that form on her porch tonight, she knew her eyes would be pried open till she crashed from sheer exhaustion. "Will you call me if the police find anything or do I need to wait for one of them?"

"I'll convince Housley to let me call."

Emmy liked that promise. They walked to the entryway without saying anything. Josh opened the door and pivoted to face her. "Dinner, tomorrow?"

Her face actually hurt she grinned so big. Maybe tonight she could lie awake dreaming about Josh, to heck with the dang murderer. "Perfect. I don't have rehearsal."

"I know, I checked."

"With who?"

"Madison Parker."

"She's a doll. One of my students."

"One of my neighbors." He smiled, but shifted his weight a few times and clung to the doorframe as if asking for much more than dinner. "Is six okay?"

"Perfect."

He gave her one more smile before striding out the door. Emmy watched as he walked out of her porch's circle of light and then down the street. Did he live close enough that he didn't have to drive, or was he going to find his police buddies and keep searching for prints? He'd never given her flashlight back.

She closed the door, dead-bolted it, and reset the alarm system. She might not be able to go to sleep, but at least tonight she'd have something pleasant to picture as she lay awake.

❧

Kelton frowned at her from his perch next to the piano. "Are you messing with me or what?"

Emmy glanced up at him. "Messing with you?"

"You never make stinking mistakes. You play perfect. You sing perfect. And today you're like a joke. Banging on the keys, playing too hard, too soft, hitting wrong notes, not even correcting me when I'm off. What is *up*?"

"Sorry. Maybe we should just call it a day." Emmy sighed, studying the white and black keys. She'd stayed up late waiting for Josh's call after listening to the police and their dog outside her back windows. He'd told her they found nothing. She should've been disappointed. Instead she'd just been thrilled at the sound of his voice and the anticipation of going out with him.

Kelton lowered his bulk next to her. Emmy slid to the side so she wouldn't be squished. "You dragging again, girl?"

"No, actually. I'm doing pretty good."

"Then why the drama?"

Emmy held up her fingers, they were obviously shaking. "Nerves."

Kelton stared at her strangely. "Nerves? Around me? I'm just your chill neighbor. You told me yourself I was too young." He broke into a wide grin. "Hold up. You saying there's a chance?"

Emmy quickly shook her head. "No."

"Slammed again." His lower lip jutted out. "What are you nervous for then?"

She took a long breath and exhaled with the words, "I've got a date tonight."

Kelton jumped and banged his knee on the piano. "Ouch. Dang. Who?"

"Josh Campbell," she whispered into the keys.

"Captain Campbell?" Kelton whistled, rubbing at his knee. "I hate to admit this, but if I can't have you I think he's pretty boss. He'd treat you right and take good care of you."

"Kelton." Emmy shook her head. "I'm going out on a date with him, not proposing."

"I get ya, slow it down. I hear it from the girls all the time."

"Oh, I bet you do." Emmy laughed, hard. "Wasn't it you who told me, 'I don't look for girls, they come to me.'"

"Ha! I did say that." His mouth twisted in a smirk. "Well, they come, but the ones I really fall for are all like, 'I'm too young to get serious. I need to finish college first." He stuck out his tongue. "Excuses, excuses."

"Those are the smart ones," Emmy advised. "The ones worth waiting for. You aren't, um, you know?"

"Getting too friendly? Nah. My momma would drown me herself if I ever pushed *that* before marriage."

"You're a good boy, Kelton."

"Thanks. Now I feel like a puppy you just patted on the head for not peeing on the carpet." He rubbed his large hands together. "But you and Campbell? I like it. What are you wearing?"

Emmy laughed. "Have I ever told you you're one of my best friends?"

He placed a hand on his heart. His dark skin crinkling as he grinned. "No, really?"

"Serious."

"No, you're really that lonely?"

Emmy shoved him but he barely moved an inch. "Get your butt back up and start singing for me, boy."

"You do realize the racial slurs you just used? If I tell my momma..."

Emmy paled. "You know I would never."

He roared with laughter. "I know. I just love to give you smack."

Emmy punched him on the shoulder. He leapt to his feet. "Okay, I'm singing, I'm singing, just play it right. And tonight, wear your blue dress, the one that shows off your shoulders with your hair up." He pretended to flip his hair off his neck. "And tomorrow, I want dirt on that date."

Chapter Fourteen

JOSH PICKED EMMY UP in the most amazing restored truck. She gushed over the red pickup, though she had no clue what year it might be or how much it was probably worth. The creamy leather seats were as soft as baby's skin and the dials and knobs a beautiful mahogany.

After turning pink under her constant praise, Josh finally admitted that his father was a mechanic and had taught him to restore old vehicles when he was only fourteen. Now he did it as a side job.

She sat across the table from him at The Driftwood Restaurant. The large windows gave a terrific view of the beach, but Emmy couldn't see anything beyond Josh. She wondered if he was nervous or if it was just her. He smiled and asked her questions about acting and the theater, but she could've sworn his hand trembled when he picked up his glass. She also noticed the shy way he glanced at her—glances that set her heart thumping.

The waitress delivered her salmon and his steak. Emmy decided she'd talked about herself enough. "Where are you from originally?" she asked.

Josh swallowed a bite and started cutting his next before answering, "I grew up in Meridian, Idaho."

"Did you work there as a firefighter?"

He nodded. "I volunteered through college at Boise State and then started full-time after I graduated."

"What did you graduate in? Is there a firefighter bachelor's degree?"

"Fire Science." He studied his utensils. "But I graduated in history."

"History? Interesting." She leaned back in her chair.

"Interesting, but not really a career. Ask my dad." He shrugged. "I hoped to teach, but after my student teaching stint, I realized I loved being a firefighter more. When I was offered a job with the fire department before any teaching positions opened up, it seemed like fate."

"So what brought you here?"

Josh regarded her thoughtfully. "Do you want the truth?"

"Nah. Lie to me." She laughed. "Of course I want the truth."

He smiled, but it slid away as he concentrated on his steak and veggies. "I got divorced and wanted to escape."

"The memories?" she guessed, sliding her hand along the condensation on her water glass.

"That and..." he grinned, "my mom kept setting me up on dates with any woman who had hair and a job. I got the opportunity to transfer here. It's a much smaller department, but included a promotion to Captain. I ran."

Emmy hadn't ever thought about Josh being married before she met him. In her mind, he'd just been there waiting for her. What a selfish thing to imagine. "Hair and a job are important." She speared a bite of salmon, savoring the buttery flavor.

He chuckled. "Yes, but it makes for some interesting

nights when the women you're dating are handpicked from your mother's salon."

Emmy pushed her broccoli around. "Aha. That makes more sense. Lots of hair then?"

"I've seen it all—dyed, permed, highlighted, crimped—you name it." He tore off a chunk of bread.

Emmy laughed, wishing she knew him well enough to ask why he got divorced. "Nice. So your mom might not approve, I've never been dyed, permed, or anything exciting."

Josh's eyes swept over her hair and face. The intensity of his gaze made her catch a breath and hold it. "My mom would approve. Natural beauty is a rare thing."

Emmy bit at her cheek. Her face flushed. "Thank you."

Dinner progressed smoothly as they took time to learn about each other and tease a bit. Emmy was grateful that the conversation never went to her past. Josh was careful not to dredge up the memories of Grayson's death. She was also happy she stopped shaking and settled down to eat the delicious food.

As they exited the restaurant, he took her hand and Emmy felt the oddest sensation—the comfort of home intermingled with such excitement she got butterflies. The ride home passed too quickly, and before she knew it, they were standing on her doorstep.

Josh leaned close, and her breath caught in her throat. He brushed the hair from her face then framed her cheek with his large palm. "Thank you for going with me," he whispered.

"Thank you for dinner," Emmy stammered, unable to think straight with his blue gaze searing through her.

He pressed his lips to her cheek. Fire raced through her and she had to force herself not to turn into the kiss. He backed away, his hand dropping to his side. His smile made

86

her breathing even more erratic. "Could I stop by tomorrow after work?"

She nodded several times.

"It might be kind of late."

"I don't sleep."

A question lit his eyes. "Not that late, maybe about nine."

Emmy blushed. "Sounds great. I'll see you then." She gave him a little wave before unlocking the door and letting herself in. Leaning around the sidelight she watched him walk to his truck, wishing he wouldn't have been such a gentleman by only kissing her cheek.

Chapter Fifteen

EMMY WAS HOME FROM PRACTICE by eight. The minutes slowly clicked by. Finally at nine-fifteen the doorbell rang. She rushed to the door. Josh stood there with a huge smile showing off his dimples. He held out his hand. "Wanna take a walk on the beach?"

Emmy had a hard time thinking with his large hand engulfing her smaller one. "Sure."

She set the alarm and locked her door with the code. Josh walked slowly, his thumb tracing across the back of her hand. Emmy trembled, his touch doing odd things to her insides. The sun had just set. Emmy loved the beach this time of night—the seagulls settling down, the waves crashing softly, and few people. It was a little bit chilly, but she hardly noticed that with Josh's warmth next to her.

"I miss walking on the beach at night."

"Did you used to walk on the beach a lot?" he asked.

"Almost every night; Grayson knew I loved it." His hand clenched hers tighter and the thumb stopped its provocative movements. She sighed. "But I haven't dared since."

Josh didn't say anything until they were almost to the water's edge. They were the only ones on the beach, and it was growing dark with only a sliver of a moon rising. He tugged her around to face him and wrapped his free arm around her back. "If you'd let me, I'd take you on a walk on the beach every night."

Emmy stared up into his deep blue eyes, mesmerized. He didn't move and seemed to be holding his breath just like she was. "I'd like that a lot," she whispered.

Josh's smile came out. Emmy gasped at the beauty of this man. His tanned skin crinkled around his mouth and the corners of his sapphire eyes. And dang if those dimples didn't reveal themselves. Emmy leaned closer without meaning to.

"Do you feel it too?" Josh whispered, closing the small gap between them until she could almost taste the warmth and manliness of him.

"What?" she asked, feeling so many things right now she wasn't sure how to distinguish one from another—attraction, desire, safety—all intermingling into a pull she couldn't fight if she wanted to.

"The...feeling between us. I've never been drawn to someone like this." He traced his fingers down her cheek, his hand on her back urging her closer. Their bodies were in full contact, their lips inches apart as he leaned down.

She studied his full lips and had to agree that whatever lured her to him was a completely new and amazing experience. "Yes," she admitted. "I feel it."

He was tantalizingly close, but he didn't move, and her breath quickened in anticipation. His eyes searched hers, and just like that night she hit her head, he was questioning. "Emmy?"

"Please," she whispered back.

He gave a brief grin before covering the distance. His mouth worked in rhythm with hers, producing the most amazing sensation. The attraction that had almost overwhelmed her before now melded into the perfect combination of joy and desire. Emmy wrapped her arms around his broad back, pulling him closer, if that were possible.

He lifted her onto her toes, deepening the kiss until she moaned with pleasure. She lost herself completely in the kiss, the way he tasted of toothpaste, the way his hands moved almost hungrily over her back, nothing mattered but Josh. He finally lowered her back onto her feet, broke contact, and just held her close, his cheek resting against her hair.

"Oh, Emmy." He groaned softly and lifted her chin until she stared into those blue eyes. "I've never—"

He didn't finish the sentence but captured her mouth again. Much, much later he broke away and Emmy took long, deep breaths, trying to clear her mind of this lightheaded, happy sensation. Josh was sweeping her away faster than any ocean current could. She loved the way he said he'd never, but then she realized, she'd never, ever felt this way about anyone. Not even her husband. That thought was like being dumped in the cold ocean. She started shivering, despite the warmth of Josh's strong embrace.

"I'd better go back," she murmured against his chest.

"Oh." He pulled away slightly so he could study her. "Okay." He ran his hands down her arms. "Are you cold?"

Emmy's teeth began chattering. She'd just gone through the most exhilarating experience of her life, and the guilt over never responding like this to Grayson as well as the loss of Josh's lips on hers had her shivering like a recovering addict.

"Emmy?" Josh held her at arm's length. "Are you okay?"

"No," she admitted.

"What's wrong?" His eyes clouded, his mouth turned down. "I shouldn't have kissed you, I moved too fast."

"No!" His kiss was something she'd cherish, though it was the cause of her inner turmoil.

He smiled softly. "I'm glad you don't regret it already."

"I don't think I'll ever regret that kiss." She attempted a smile but it came out lopsided.

"What is it, Sweetheart? You can tell me."

His term of endearment pushed her over the edge. She buried her head in his chest as tears crested her eyelids. Josh held her close until she stopped quivering. Finally she gained enough composure to look up at him.

"What is it? I'll be here for you, Emmy."

She shook her head. "You terrify me, Josh."

"What?" His arms dropped to his side. His eyes widened.

Emmy worked to control her breathing, but her breaths were coming faster and faster as she fought the tears that wanted to surface. "I've never felt like that before. I want to be with you so much it's a physical ache."

Josh smiled and reached out to her again.

Emmy held up a hand. "You've got to give me time to process all of this. It feels better than...Christmas to be in your arms. It's the most amazing sensation in the world."

He studied her with a solemn expression. "And that's a bad thing?"

"I'm scared," she finally admitted. "Scared that you're just some shooting star. You're going to burn out and leave me."

"What? You're not making sense. I've been waiting, just hoping you'd feel the way I do. Even before I met you officially, I couldn't get you out of my mind."

"But that's just the problem. It's all...wrong. I was attracted to you when I was married."

He inhaled sharply.

"You see why I feel so guilty?"

Josh blinked quickly as if trying to dispel the image. Finally he whispered, "My wife cheated on me. When I found out you were married, I did everything in my power to forget about you. I swore I'd never be the kind of person to break up a marriage."

Emmy licked her lips and placed her hand on his forearm. "I'm so sorry." She hung her head, dropping her hand. "I tried everything to make my marriage good, but honestly Josh...it never felt like this. What if this magic between us dims and I can't bring it back?" *Like I couldn't create it with Grayson?*

Josh studied her for several uncomfortable seconds. "Emmy, even if you felt something for me when you were married, you didn't act on it. In fact, you bit my head off when I approached you."

Emmy blushed. "I remember that."

"Me too." He stepped closer and held out his hand.

It was such a kind invitation, not pushy, not trying to re-incite the passion, just being there for her. Emmy grasped his fingers, warmth spreading through her at the intimacy of even this small touch.

"We don't have to have all the answers. We've both been through hard things. But I do know that I want to get to know you better. I want you in my life."

Emmy smiled.

"Can we at least give us a try and see what happens?"

Emmy was pretty sure fireworks were going to happen

when he looked at her like she was the only thing that mattered to him. A try could lead to so much more. She wasn't sure if she was ready for that but found herself nodding.

They continued their walk along the beach. Josh shared more about his childhood and how he'd recovered from his brief marriage. Emmy didn't know what to make of her overly-active hormones when she looked at, thought about, or touched this man, but she did know he was an extremely good person and she wanted to get to know him better.

Chapter Sixteen

EMMY CARESSED THE PIANO KEYS, playing Claire de Lune for the thousandth time. Rain fell softly outside, muting the world and creating a bubble where the music floated her away from her fear and worries. She became so lost in the familiar notes that she daydreamed about Josh. She couldn't wait to see him again, but at the same time she worried. She'd never imagined kissing someone could feel that amazing. What if it was just temporary sizzle and sparks? She wanted the comfortable, safe love she had with Grayson, but she also wanted something more. They were different men. Couldn't she have a different relationship with Josh without losing her love for Grayson, without betraying his memories?

Her fingers stilled on the keys at the end of the song. She sat there, the silence drifting over her. A tapping just a bit louder than the rain on the back patio yanked her from her relaxed state. Someone was out there. Could have been out there the entire time she played. Could have been listening to her. Her hands grew clammy against the piano.

She wanted to call the police and cower under a blanket until they came, but her legs were in motion before her brain caught up. She exploded across the living room, flung open the back door, and searched the murky evening. She couldn't see anyone, but he was there. She knew it.

She screamed into the night. "I'm not afraid of you! You hear me? You killed my husband, but you can't make me afraid!"

The shrill house alarm split the air and Emmy jumped. She knew whoever had been there would be long gone, but she was still going to try to find him. Ignoring a young couple on the beach watching her like she should be in the loony bin, she slammed and dead-bolted the door, then called the security company and the police. She wasn't going to let fear control her any longer.

🐾

Emmy giggled as she watched the bar scene with Gaston and his cronies play out on the stage—her stage. They sang too loudly and thought themselves hilarious. It was great. Kelton was absolutely perfect as Gaston.

A throat cleared at her side. "Emmy?"

She turned to see Shane towering over her. His dark hair was combed back and his beard had been trimmed. She smiled. "You've done a fabulous job with the sets, Shane. Thank you."

He revealed crooked teeth with a soft grin. "I'm so glad you like them."

"I do." She turned back to the stage. He stood next to her until she grew a bit uncomfortable. "Is there anything else you need?"

"Would you like to go to Mo's after practice with me?"

Emmy took a slow breath. She had to let him down easy because she couldn't replace him at the theater. He was such a nice man, always taking care of the actors' needs and never looking for a thank you.

"No, I can't." She hated the pained look in his eyes and rushed on, "It's just too soon. I haven't recovered from..." She swallowed and looked away. She was such a liar. She'd recovered enough to think about Josh nonstop and to kiss him. But lying was better than hurting Shane's feelings.

His shoulders slumped. "I understand, but when you're ready, I'll be here."

He held her gaze for a moment longer before turning and shuffling toward backstage. Emmy refocused on the raucous singing, wishing she could've avoided that entire interaction.

Chapter Seventeen

JOSH WATCHED THE THEATER ENTRANCE through a soft drizzle, anxious for the moment Emmy would appear. He brushed the rain off his face. Was he being too forward coming to see her again so soon? He didn't want to scare her off when he knew she had reservations.

She exited the door full of happiness, gesturing with her hands and laughing at Timothy, the guy who always acted opposite her. A flash of jealousy stabbed him. She probably spent more time with Timothy than she had her husband. The actor was the epitome of tall, dark, and handsome, plus he shared her passion for performing. Emmy was not only beautiful and talented she was also wealthy. Josh was a public servant who didn't really understand her talent or social status. Did he have a chance of finding a place in her life?

Emmy clicked her keyless entry then paused before opening her door. She glanced in Josh's direction and lit up for a moment. Timothy said something and she lost her smile. She nodded to Timothy before walking purposefully to Josh's side.

"Hey. How are you?" He raised a hand in tentative greeting.

Emmy grabbed his arm and tugged him toward the side

of the building. When they were under an overhang and protected from the rain and anyone watching, she said, "What are you doing here?"

"I—" Josh stammered.

Her smooth skin wrinkled at the forehead. Her eyes shot him a questioning glance. "Listen, you can't just show up all the time. It's like you're stalking me."

His eyebrows rose. *Stalking?* He wanted to protect her and love her and she thought of him as a stalker? It was as if the kiss had never happened and they were back to zero. He was getting sick of her pushing him away every time he thought he'd made progress. "Yeah, because me and Timothy and every guy in the audience can't help ourselves so we follow you around like puppies."

She didn't respond, just elevated one shoulder. Her dark eyes full of questions.

"I'm not one of your fans who can't see straight when they're around you." Now he was lying, but he hated the jealousy eating away at him. She'd been embarrassed to see him. She probably *was* dating Timothy.

Her mouth flapped open. "I know you're not. I just thought..." He watched her face change to a lovely shade of pink. She studied the wooden planks under their feet and tucked a strand of hair behind her ear. "I'm sorry. This other guy asked me out and I lied to him and said I wasn't ready to date. Then seeing you here. I feel guilty about kissing you and," she pushed out a long breath, "enjoying it so much. I don't want to forget Grayson. I don't know if I'm ready to move on. I'm just...confused."

Josh deflated. It wasn't fair to be upset at her when she was obviously struggling, but he had no clue how to help her move passed her husband's memory. He gently touched her cheek and then tilted her chin up. "I'm sorry too. I was excited to see you again and then to have you think I'm stalking you."

She shook her head, dislodging his fingers. "I don't. It's just..." She exhaled before saying, "I'm not ready to date. I should've told you the other night. This doesn't feel right."

Josh studied her eyes as she spoke. Her words didn't match the intensity of her gaze. Of course she was an expert at acting, saying things she didn't mean, but he didn't think she was being truthful with him. He gulped, terrified that if his instincts were wrong, he would force her to reject him outright. "You're lying to me, Emmy. You like me, and it scares you."

Emmy blinked then leaned closer to him and whispered, "Josh, this isn't real. You and I are like something people dream of, something from Hollywood."

Josh smiled at that. Touching her felt better than anything Hollywood could conjure up. He'd watched her from afar and then stayed away since Grayson's death, fighting his desire to be with her. It was reassuring that she recognized the pull between them.

"I know what a real relationship is," she said. "I've been in one." Her eyes darkened and filled with pain and guilt.

Josh held her gaze; it hurt him to know the pain she was going through, missing her husband and probably feeling like she was betraying him. And it felt like his stomach was being gouged out when he thought of her with Grayson, Timothy, or anyone else.

"But you and I." She pointed at him. "We're all sparkles and tingles and that isn't real, that fizzes out. I know. I dated other men besides Grayson, and one of us would get bored and move on. I just can't do that again."

Josh's shoulders rounded, but something in her gaze told him to fight. The rain dripping off the roof insulated them in their own world. He took a step toward her and cupped her face in his palm. "Are you honestly telling me that it has ever felt this good?"

He bowed his head and captured her lips before she could protest. She returned the kiss and her assessment was dead on—sparks zinged between them, the air warmed against his skin, and every star aligned. He could've gone on kissing her all night. With super human self-control he forced himself to release her mouth. Now was not the time to push his luck. He tucked her small form into his arms and enjoyed each second.

"The connection between us is more real than anything I've ever felt!" he whispered fervently, still holding her in his arms.

Emmy stared up at him with liquid eyes. "But that's just what I'm saying. We're drawn to each other, but it's all physical. You don't really know me. The kind of relationship I want is comfortable, not some fireworks show." She stepped back and he dropped his arms.

Josh shook his head. Was she saying this because she knew Timothy so well and thought she should date him? He had to be the one who had asked her out. How could Josh convince her that although the physical attraction was huge, they were so much more than the physical? "I want what you want, Sweetheart. What we're feeling is where it starts. It's not wrong to feel like this; it's brought us together, and now we have the chance to get to know each other, to get comfortable." He smiled at her. "But I imagine when we've been together fifty years you'll still make me sizzle."

"Fifty?" Emmy bit her lip and turned away. "I'm sorry, Josh. Honestly, I'm scared of the sizzle."

She brushed by him and walked through the increasing rain to her car, not avoiding the puddles. Josh watched her go, wanting to cuss, needing to chase after her. He didn't want to give up. He cared about her too much. But was he what she wanted or needed?

Emmy risked a glance back as she drove away, shivering from the cold and emotion. The rain darkened the evening sky but she could still see Josh in the middle of the parking lot, watching her drive away. It hurt to leave him there, and her breath came in ragged gulps. She struggled to hold back the tears. She was so far out of her comfort zone—terrified to commit to a new relationship, but she liked him. She more than liked him. What was she doing calling him a stalker, claiming they could never work, and then driving away? She pressed on the gas harder when everything inside wanted to turn the car around, find Josh, and kiss him until the sparks started to dim. She smiled, wondering if they ever would. Would it be so bad to let the fires rage? What then? Then maybe she'd be alone again and she didn't know if she could survive losing something that powerful.

She turned her windshield wipers faster and searched the empty street. It would be so easy to make a U-turn. She covered three blocks alternating between pushing harder on the gas and moving her foot to the brake.

Her thoughts were interrupted by soft breathing from the backseat. Her own breath caught in her throat as she tried to decipher the noise. Was she just being paranoid, or was someone really in her Enclave?

She worked up the nerve to turn and look. A huge shadow loomed behind her. An arm came around her neck. All her breath sucked inside before it released in a loud scream.

Her foot slammed the brake pedal down. She clawed at the arm around her neck with one hand as the tires squealed against the wet asphalt.

"Keep driving." The voice was muffled and unrecognizable under the Halloween mask. The man wore long sleeves and gloves that scratched at the skin of Emmy's neck. She panted for air, jammed the car into park, and reached for her door handle. A long knife appeared between her and the door. The man yanked her against the seat with his forearm and waved the knife in her face. "I said keep driving."

Emmy's movements were sluggish, like a dream. She wanted to fight him, but could hardly make her limbs cooperate. She reached for the gearshift and slowly dropped it into drive.

"Drive toward Ecola."

She didn't know what else to do but comply. Her clammy hands gripped the steering wheel to control the trembling. Did she dare push the emergency button to make a call or would he slice her open? Her eyes flitted to the knife. It was the epitome of every nightmare she'd dealt with over the last year coming to fruition. This man had killed her husband. *With that knife.* And now he was here to kill her or worse.

She'd rather die than be subject to some psychopath who would resort to murder so they could "be together" like it said in the last note. The fear had her breath coming in short gasps and her hands were barely able to grip the steering wheel as thoughts of what he would do to her clawed through her mind.

A large boulder appeared off the right side of the road, framed against the dark forest by her headlights. Emmy didn't stop to think as she pressed the accelerator into the floor and swerved toward the rock. The man emitted a high-pitched scream. The Enclave slammed into the rock. Emmy's seatbelt held her tight as the airbag exploded in her face and the man was thrown into the windshield, his legs pinned by the passenger airbag.

Pain raced through her face and abdomen. Emmy tried to catch a full breath, knowing she had little time. She undid her seatbelt and yanked at the door latch. The door didn't open. No! She screamed and jammed her shoulder into the door. The man didn't say anything but his heavy exhales seemed to reach out to her. Again and again she slammed against the door. Finally it popped open and she fell onto the spongy ground next to her vehicle.

Her tormenter peered at her over the airbag. All she could see of his face was his dark eyes, determination seeping through the pain written there. His knife sliced through the airbag several times as he untangled himself from the wreckage. Emmy didn't wait to see what he would do next but scrambled to her feet and started running back up the highway toward Cannon Beach.

The headlights of a large vehicle, maybe a truck, came toward her. Rescue looked so far away on the long, open road. She ran down the faded yellow lines, waving her arms and screaming for help, though the vehicle's occupants couldn't possibly hear her. Between screams she heard the quick pounding of footsteps getting closer. The bright red truck skidded to a stop in front of her. Josh.

The driver's side door popped open and Emmy rushed around to him, still screaming, "Help! Help!"

Josh grabbed her in his arms and swung her off her feet. "Emmy! Are you okay?"

"No!" She glanced back and saw the dark-cloaked man coming at them. "Josh!"

He set her on her feet and spun to face the man.

"I waited a year for her," the man said in a gruff voice. "You can't have her." He stabbed at Josh.

Josh ducked under the blade and slammed his fist into the man's covered face. The man reeled back but came up fast, slicing Josh's shirt and abdomen open. Blood covered the knife.

Emmy shrieked. She launched herself at the guy's side and hit at the arm holding the knife with all her strength. The man turned to her.

Josh punched the guy in the chest and yelled, "Emmy, get back!"

Emmy dodged out of the way, wondering how Josh was still standing with blood dripping down his severed stomach. The man gasped for air but took one more swipe, barely missing Josh's left arm. Two vehicles approached from the north.

The man darted toward Emmy. She whirled away, slipping on the wet concrete and ducking his arms. People popped out of the cars. Josh moved in front of Emmy. The man took off at a run, dodging trees as he headed into the forest. Josh took two steps after him then slowly sank to his knees.

"Josh!" Emmy ran to him, ripping off her jacket and pressing it against the blood pulsing out of his body. "Oh, Josh!" Every memory of seeing Grayson sliced open resurfaced. No! This couldn't happen again. Not to Josh. *Please, Lord, help him. Help me.*

Josh's eyes held a look of panic for a second then they closed and he sagged in her arms. Emmy tried to support him but he was too heavy and they thudded onto the asphalt. Her back and arm took most of the impact. She bit down the pain, grateful Josh hadn't received any more injury.

Footsteps thudded around them. Someone tried to pull him from her arms. "No!" Emmy yelled at them. "No!" She was desperate to keep him safe. "I'm putting pressure on the wound. Just get help."

One woman was already on her phone. "The police are on their way."

Another man sat behind Emmy and helped brace her and Josh as she continued to compress the gash with every ounce of strength left. Silent tears mingled with the rain sliding down her face. Josh didn't respond. Was he already gone? Was he going to leave her like Grayson had? She couldn't survive losing him.

Chapter Eighteen

JOSH WAKENED TO A VERY SOFT HAND gripping his and a vision sitting at his bedside. She studied the monitors next to his bed like someone staring into a campfire, almost catatonic. Through the soft light of the room, he could see her dark hair hanging limp around her face, which featured black smears and puffy eyes. She was even more beautiful to him.

"Hey," he croaked.

"Josh! You're awake." She leaned forward and hugged him carefully as if he would break, pulling away much too quickly. "How do you feel?"

"Foggy." His head was full of whipped cream. The only thing that seemed lucid to him was Emmy.

"Do you hurt?"

He shook his head, glancing at his IV. "Morphine?"

"I think so."

"How bad is it?" He gestured with his chin to his abdomen.

She gave him a brave smile. "Not as bad as I thought. Lots of stitches. I think they said forty-five, but it wasn't deep, just long." She spread her hands almost a foot apart. "You lost a lot of blood, but they said you'd heal pretty quick."

Relief washed over him. He'd woken in the ambulance

106

to excruciating pain and nobody willing to tell him anything. Then they put him under as soon as he reached the hospital. "Did they find him?"

Emmy frowned. "No."

He pushed the button to raise his bed up and pain sliced through him. He gasped, obviously he wasn't ready for movement even with the morphine.

"It hurts? Oh, Josh. I'm so sorry."

He forced himself to smile to reassure Emmy and took a couple of long breaths as well as a sip of the water she offered him before managing to say, "You shouldn't be sorry."

"You got hurt protecting me."

Josh gave her a genuine smile. "It was worth it."

"You're crazy, you know that?" But she was smiling.

"Crazy for you."

Emmy blushed becomingly. "I like it when you flirt with me."

He wished with everything in him that he wasn't wounded in a hospital bed and could show her how crazy he was for her. "I just like you."

She grinned. "I'm beginning to see that."

They smiled at each other for several seconds. Josh hated that his brain was murky and he couldn't think of anything cute to say to her. He shifted position again and winced.

"Oh, Josh." Emmy gripped his hand. "I'm so sorry he hurt you."

"There you go again, being sorry for something that isn't your fault."

She laughed but sobered quickly. "Do you remember what happened?"

"Yeah." He especially remembered when the guy had

almost grabbed Emmy before running off. What if he'd taken her? Josh had to be able to protect her, and he was stuck in a hospital bed. "They couldn't find him?"

Emmy looked at him with such concern, but thankfully didn't withhold information. "He was smart. They followed his tracks through the woods. The prints disappeared at a stream and they think he headed west to the ocean. Nobody knows how long he stayed in the water. They couldn't find his prints leaving. They think he exited barefoot on a busy part of the beach so all the footprints and smells could intermingle."

Josh wanted to swear. He nodded instead. "Did he seem familiar to you at all?"

"I keep trying to remember, but I was so scared. All I could think about was him not hurting you." She exhaled. "I noticed he has dark eyes and he's as tall as you."

"You did great, Sweetheart."

"Thank you." She squeezed his hand then released it. "Do you want more water?"

"Yes, please." He took a long drink and leaned back against the pillows. "What time is it?"

"About four a.m."

"You sat here all night?"

"Yes." She looked at him indignantly. "You'd do the same for me."

Josh loved that she knew that and that she had done it for him.

"Why'd you follow me?" she asked.

Josh shifted on the bed, this time doing a better job at hiding the pain. "I wish I could say I was some sort of altruistic hero, but I was mad at you for running away. I decided I'd follow you. When you didn't go home, I stayed back a little ways so you wouldn't get spooked." He shrugged. "I'm glad I was there."

Emmy shuddered. "Me too. And don't you ever say you're not a hero. You're my hero."

Josh had to fight a smile at her passionate declaration. "I wish I had a toothbrush so I could ask for a kiss."

Emmy grinned and kissed his cheek softly. "As strong as our attraction is I'd probably rip your stitches open."

His eyebrows arched. "Oh? I'd like to try that."

"No, you wouldn't!"

He didn't refute her, but he definitely would. He swallowed down the nasty taste in his mouth before growing brave enough to ask, "Did you decide you're willing to give us a try?"

"I thought he'd killed you." She coughed and blinked a few times before continuing, "I realized I could lose you at any time, and it's absolute stupidity to stay away when you're exactly who I want to be with."

Josh studied her for a few seconds. Her beautiful face lit up with what he hoped was love for him. He knew it was what he felt inside. He pushed the call button on his bed.

"Yes?" a voice answered.

"Can you please bring me a toothbrush? There's a beautiful lady visiting me, and I really need to kiss her."

Practice had gone late and Emmy was exhausted from too many sleepless nights. Her alarm system should've reassured her, but every noise awoke new fears. She also worried about the murderer going after Josh, who didn't have a fancy security system or the police patrolling his neighborhood. No one else seemed to think he was in the danger she was.

She wished they'd catch the murderer so she could have a normal life—teaching, acting, swimming, and spending every spare minute with Josh. She dragged her toes, studying the pavement as she made her way to the rented Camry—with pepper spray in one hand and her cell phone in the other. She wanted her Enclave back. She wanted her peace of mind back more.

"Emmy?" A voice said right behind her.

She jumped and whirled, placing a hand on her heart. "Oh, Shane, you scared me!"

He offered a shy smile. "I'm sorry. I would never want to scare you."

Emmy wished so many things didn't scare her. She hoped he wasn't going to ask her out again and preempted him with, "I love the staircase of the Beast's castle. Thank you for working so hard."

"I'm happy to do it for you."

Emmy forced a smile, but didn't like his wording. He wasn't doing it for *her*. "Thank you." She turned. "I'd better get home. Exhausting practice today."

"Could I take you to dinner tomorrow?" His words flew out before she could escape.

Emmy bit her cheek. What should she say? "I'm sorry, Shane. It's not a good time for me to date someone."

He studied her intently, all traces of a smile gone. "When will be a good time?"

Emmy shook her head. She needed to be honest. "I don't know. I'm involved with someone else right now." She had to hide a smile thinking of her personal hero. "Thank you for asking."

He nodded but didn't respond. The silence grew awkward.

A police car pulled up next to them. "Are you doing okay, Mrs. Henderson?"

Emmy turned to them with a reassuring smile. "Yes. Thank you for checking. This is Shane, he's the prop manager here at the theater."

"He knows me," Shane muttered.

Emmy didn't know how to respond to that. The police had questioned and searched everyone who worked at the theater after Grayson's death. What a relief it wasn't one of her fellow actors who killed her husband.

The officer nodded to Shane then looked at Emmy. "We're always watching out for you, ma'am."

"Thank you." It was a nice reassurance, but they couldn't be around all the time. At some point the knife-wielding lunatic was going to reappear. She shivered at the thought.

The police car idled next to them. She glanced up to see Shane studying her. "I'll see you tomorrow," Emmy said and then walked away, more uncomfortable than she'd felt in a long time. She opened the back door of the Camry and checked behind the seats, then opened the driver's side and settled in. A quick wave to the police and she was happy to drive away from the uncomfortable situation with Shane. She was also grateful when she saw the police had followed her.

Chapter Nineteen

MOVEMENT ON THE BACK PATIO drew Emmy's eyes from her book and pushed her heart rate into overdrive. Was it the murderer? Would he try to break into her house, or would he run away again? She dialed 911 as she cautiously crept to the sliding glass doors. Edging back the curtain, she flipped on the light.

"911. What's your emergency?"

"Kelton!" Emmy screamed. She disabled the alarm and yanked open the door.

"Kelton?" the woman on the phone asked.

"I'm sorry, ma'am. It was a mistake. I'm fine."

Kelton stood grinning at her as she went through twenty questions with the operator, assuring her that she'd just been spooked by her teenage neighbor. Emmy hung up the phone and crossed her arms over her chest. "What are you doing?"

Kelton gestured to a cot and sleeping bag. "I'm camping out."

"Why?"

The grin slid off his face. "I'm not letting that guy hurt you, Em."

Emmy shook her head, the anger sliding away. "Oh, Kelton. You can't do this."

"I am doing this."

112

"If you haven't noticed, the man doesn't seem to want to kill me. He wants to kill any other guy who cares about me."

Kelton's cocky grin was back. "Let the dude try and come at me." He motioned to his pile of supplies, which included treats, as if this were a fun campout, and a long lacrosse stick. "I can be vicious with this thing."

Emmy half-laughed. "I've seen that, but this isn't a game, and this guy is not going to give you time to get your stick in your hand when he comes at you with a knife." She shivered just thinking about it and dialed Abby's cell phone number.

A few minutes later Tyrell had marched a furious Kelton home and Emmy was back in her dead-bolted, alarm-activated house. She couldn't help smiling at the sweetness of Kelton trying to watch out for her, but the thought of that guy coming after her neighbor with his knife removed the smile from her face and filled her with dread.

Chapter Twenty

EMMY'S MOUTH WATERED AS SHE LIFTED the serving platter filled with lemon chicken, stir-fried veggies, and shrimp-fried rice from the back seat of her car. She balanced the tray on one arm and knocked on Josh's black front door, glancing at the patrol car that had followed her from home.

Josh swung the door open a few seconds later. His grin got so wide she was able to savor the dimples on display and the warmth in his blue eyes. He wore sweats and nothing else, his broad chest and defined abdomen marred by bandages, but her mouth still went dry and her face flushed.

"What did I do to deserve this?"

Emmy tilted her head to the side as if debating. "I'm not sure...maybe fighting to save my life and getting knifed?"

Josh stepped out of her way, gesturing her inside. "This smells good enough, maybe I'll try for another knife fight."

Emmy's smile froze. "That wasn't funny."

He placed a warm hand on her back. "You're right, it wasn't." He guided her through the living room into a well-organized kitchen with big windows, antique white cabinets, robin's egg blue walls, and a cozy two-person table.

Emmy set the food down.

"Will you stay and eat with me?" Josh peered over her shoulder at the abundant spread.

She turned and found herself face to chest, and oh what a chest it was. She swallowed and licked her lips. "Sure. I think this is one of those times that my food actually turned out."

"I'm sure your food always turns out." He brushed some hair away from her face.

Emmy watched the muscles in his shoulder bulge then forced herself to look into his eyes instead of ogling him. "No. But that's what I get for never following a recipe."

"A recipe would interfere with your natural artistic abilities."

"Exactly." Emmy smiled, loving that he got that so easily. Grayson had teased her about sometimes failing in the kitchen and asked her repeatedly to use a recipe. As always when she found herself comparing the two of them, Emmy felt a rush of guilt.

"Excuse me for a second." Josh walked down a short hallway and disappeared into a bedroom. She heard his grunt of pain before he came back with a baggy T-shirt on.

"You didn't have to get dressed for me." Emmy blushed at exposing her desire, knowing how out of line she was to want him uncovered.

"My mom would kill me if I ate dinner with a lady without a shirt on."

Emmy smiled. She'd like to meet his mom. She had always loved Grayson's mom, but their phone calls were growing shorter and farther apart.

The food was every bit as wonderful as Emmy had hoped. She was savoring a bite of the zesty lemon chicken when Josh turned the conversation to her. "You know a lot about me and I don't even know where you grew up."

She swallowed and took a long sip of water before

answering, "Detroit."

"And where did you learn to sing and act?"

"My aunt paid for years of private lessons. When my mom died she made me go to American Conservatory Theater for a Masters in Performing Arts." She couldn't look at him. She wanted to share with him and get to know him, but it was just so painful to talk about. You'd think as an adult you wouldn't need your mom, but she missed her all the time.

"I'm sorry to hear about your mom."

"Thank you." She focused on her plate, really not wanting to talk about it.

"What happened?"

"Cancer."

Josh pulled in a quick breath. "That's tough."

Emmy clutched her napkin. "Yes, it was."

"You got your masters in Detroit?"

"No. San Francisco." Emmy breathed a sigh of relief that he didn't ask more about her mom.

"So you moved to California for graduate school?"

"No, I moved there earlier."

"Emmy?" He set his fork down and lifted her chin with his fingers.

Her breath came in short puffs as her skin tingled from his touch. She forced herself to be brave and look at him.

"What's wrong? What don't you want to tell me?"

She twisted the paper napkin in her lap until it shredded. "I didn't have the great American childhood."

Josh blinked. "What does that mean?"

She studied the fabulous food that was growing cold. It didn't matter as she'd eaten plenty, and this conversation would've ruined her appetite even if she was famished. Josh's

116

plate was nearly empty. "Are you done? Let me clean up." She stood. "Where do you keep your Tupperware? You can eat this tomorrow."

Josh didn't say anything as he found storage containers and helped her clean up. He grunted when he bent down to look in a lower cabinet and cringed when he had to reach up.

"Please, go sit down. I can clean this up quick."

"Normally I'd fight you on that, but I am really tired."

Emmy gave him a forced smile. He looked at her with such concern before walking out of the kitchen. She watched him go. Even injured and disheveled, he was the most handsome man she'd ever known.

Emmy shook her head, fighting tears for some reason. He was so kind to not pry when she wasn't ready to share, but she almost wished he would. He'd risked his life for her, and she was falling for him fast. She wanted to confide in him and have it over with.

It would be so easy to be with him, to just let it all go, and ask him to hold her as they talked. Instead, she took her time putting away the food, washing the dishes by hand, and scrubbing the small table and counter several times. She stacked the dishes she'd brought on the table and forced herself to walk into the other room.

Josh sat on the leather couch, resting his head against the tan wall behind him. Emmy wondered why he wasn't in the huge recliner, the couch seemed too small for his long frame. His eyes opened at the sound of her approach. He blinked, smiled, and patted the spot next to him. "Thank you again for dinner and for cleaning up. It was the best food I've had in a long time."

Emmy sank down next to him, fighting the urge to

cuddle into his side. She'd probably hurt his stitches and declare her undying devotion. Neither a good idea. She clasped her hands together, inhaling that unique blend of musk and salt.

Josh reached over and covered her hands with his large fingers. Emmy unclasped her hands, turned her left hand over, and interlaced their fingers. She glanced up at him. His grin told her she'd done a good thing.

She leaned closer and he bent his head to capture her mouth with his. Emmy lost all track of time and rational thought. She savored each movement of his lips and his hands in her hair and around her waist. She wanted him closer. She wrapped her arms around his shoulders, pulling herself against his chest. He moaned. She recognized it wasn't a moan of passion and jerked back. "Oh, Josh. Your stitches. I'm so sorry."

"I'll take a little pain for a kiss like that any day." His eyes were lit with a mischievousness she loved.

Emmy's face filled with color. "I would take the kiss too, but not if it meant hurting you."

"I'm tough."

"Well, I can see that!" She threw her hands in the air when his grin broadened. "Never mind. How about we hold off on the kissing until you're feeling better?"

His eyes widened. "Why would we do something stupid like that? I don't care if you bump into my stitches."

"Well, I do! I obviously can't control myself when you start kissing me."

Josh chuckled. "That's the best thing I've ever heard."

Emmy blushed deeper. What was she going to admit to next? "I'm not saying anything right, maybe I'd better go." She started to stand.

Josh tugged on her hand. "Please, don't. I love having you here with me."

Emmy loved being here. The house was clean and masculine and one of the few places she felt completely safe. But she also knew how attracted she was to Josh. She didn't want to hurt his wound or do something she might regret.

She sat back down next to him. He held her hand softly and asked, "Tell me all about you. Please?"

Emmy stiffened. "Do you really need to know?"

"Yes." He gave her a lingering kiss then leaned back and grinned. "You admitted at the hospital that you want to be with me. A guy with a knife couldn't chase me away. You might as well tell me all your secrets."

"What if my secrets make you run?"

Josh's warm gaze on her face felt better than a tropical breeze. "Oh, Em. Nothing you could say would make me run." He lifted their clasped hands and kissed her fingers. "Nothing."

Emmy covered the distance, pressing her lips to his to show how much she loved his response. She tried to hold back so she wouldn't hurt his stitches again, but the intensity and attraction merged perfectly with the love she felt for and from him. When they finally broke apart she gasped for air.

She took several deep breaths, pushed her hair back over her shoulder, and studied their interlocked fingers.

"Talk or I'll kiss it out of you."

Emmy grinned. "I'll take the latter, please."

He gave her a tender kiss before reclining into the sofa and pulling her against his shoulder. "Did it work?"

Emmy nodded. She licked her lips then plunged ahead,

beginning with her childhood, or rather lack of a childhood, growing up hungry and destitute in Detroit. She shared her ache for a complete family and how her mother had tried to make things fun when she wasn't working, how hard it had been to watch her suffer through the cancer treatments and then waste away. As she talked, he rubbed her fingers.

He responded kindly, asking questions to flesh out the story. When she got to teenage years and her best friend, Grayson, Josh gripped her hand tighter. Though he nodded encouragingly, she could tell it was difficult for him.

"Grayson wanted to get me away from my aunt and the theater in L.A. We moved to Cannon Beach right after our honeymoon in Tahiti."

Josh actually flinched.

"Sorry," she said. "This has to be hard for you."

"No." He shook his head. "Okay, yes, but just because I'm selfish and want you all to myself."

"You've got me all to yourself."

He kissed the side of her mouth, whispering against her lips, "Sorry for being selfish."

She swallowed hard, staring into the blue eyes that completely captivated her. "I get it. I don't like to think about you being with your ex-wife."

"Good to know you understand some of my jealousy." He smiled. "But there's a difference. I have no desire to be with my ex-wife, that choice was taken from you and Grayson."

Emmy sighed heavily. He was right, and the remorse she sometimes felt when she ached to be with Josh but still didn't know how to let go of Grayson was like being under a heavy blanket on a hundred degree day.

"I'd better get going." She stood, and he didn't tug her back down. Retrieving her dishes from the kitchen, Emmy walked toward the front door.

Josh met her there. "Housley will be here in a second to follow you home."

Emmy nodded her thanks, knowing he would not only follow her home but check inside her house and garage. She appreciated how diligent they were with her safety, but she longed for the innocence of life before Grayson's murder.

Josh trailed a hand down her face and cupped her chin with his strong fingers. "I know this is hard."

Tears pricked at the corners of her eyes. She refused to let them fall. All she wanted was to spend every minute getting to know him, kissing him, becoming a couple, but was she ready for that kind of commitment? She wanted to be.

"We'll get through it." Josh's eyes darkened to a midnight blue, filled with determination.

Emmy had to blink back the tears again. "We?"

He tilted her chin up and bent his head, giving her a soft kiss. "Yes, we."

"So we are a we?" She couldn't stop a laugh at how silly that sounded.

"The best we I've ever been a part of." Josh kissed her again. This time it was not soft and it was not short. Emmy savored it, hoping she could stay a part of this we for a long, long time.

Chapter Twenty-one

JOSH CALLED THE NEXT MORNING and asked Emmy to lunch at Mo's. Grinning at the mirror, she finished applying mascara and did a little twirl in her white sundress. She couldn't wait to be with him again. The doorbell rang and she danced down the stairs to get it.

"Josh—" Her smile dropped as she realized who was on her doorstep. "Aunt Jalina?"

Her aunt wrapped her up in her fleshy arms then screamed over her shoulder, "Carl, hurry up!"

Uncle Carl moved as fast as his bony, arthritic body would allow. Emmy pulled from Jalina's embrace and rushed down the stairs to hug her uncle.

"Oh, Darlin'," he whispered. "How are you?"

"I'm doing wonderful." She smiled up at him. "It's so good to see you." She had to blink quickly to hide the tears. Uncle Carl may have been the only one left who knew everything about her and loved her just the same.

Josh's truck pulled up to the curb and Emmy felt her smile grow. Well, maybe there was one more person who was getting to know her that well and might even love her.

"What is this nonsense about you being accosted?" Aunt Jalina shrieked.

Emmy cringed and tried to keep a positive expression on her face. Why couldn't Jalina have come to visit just to say hi? "I'm fine, Auntie."

Josh descended carefully from the truck and walked across the lawn to them. Emmy held out a hand. "Josh saved me."

She beamed at him and filled with warmth as he took her hand and gave her one of his dimpled smiles. He wore jeans and a baggy Mo's t-shirt that said, "Bite me."

Carl's lined face welcomed Josh. He extended his hand. Josh released Emmy's hand to shake with her uncle. "Thank you for protecting our girl," Carl said.

Jalina's expression puckered like she'd just eaten a lemon, rind and all. "*Who* are you?"

Josh turned to her aunt and extended his hand. "Josh Campbell. Nice to meet you, ma'am."

Jalina inhaled slowly and glared at him. "So this man saved you, Emmaline? What is he, a gardener or a pool boy?"

Josh looked confused; his hand dropped to the side.

Emmy reached for his hand and held it in both of hers. Her aunt was not snubbing *her* man. "Josh is a firefighter, Aunt Jalina. A hero in every sense of the word and my personal hero."

Josh smiled uneasily at her.

Jalina tilted her chin up. "I can see that you might be smitten by his looks, but you have no right to turn your back on your upbringing and start dating a common man who would wear a T-shirt like that." She pointed a squishy hand.

Emmy straightened. "You cannot even understand how superior Josh is. He's wearing a loose T-shirt because he almost got killed protecting me two nights ago and anything fitted would rub on his stitches!"

Jalina nodded. "Like I said, we really appreciate Josh saving you, but you need to think about how hard it would be to have a relationship with someone who is obviously below your social status. He could never provide for you like Grayson has."

Josh tried to pull his hand out of Emmy's. She clamped down tighter on his fingers. "I am completely capable of providing for myself, and you know as well as anybody that I don't give a snot about social status! Josh is the man I am choosing to date. You can get behind that choice or you can leave."

Uncle Carl lifted his hands. "Now, Jalina, don't go driving a wedge."

She turned the force of her scowl on him. "She's driving the wedge! We are leaving!" She marched toward the car, muttering, "Ungrateful little brat, gave her everything and she turns her nose up at me."

Uncle Carl shook his head and gave them a sad smile. "It was nice to meet you, Josh, take good care of my girl, will you?"

Josh swallowed and nodded. "I will, Sir."

Emmy gave her uncle another hug. He whispered into her ear, "Don't let her bother you, Darlin', she'll get over it. She just throws these fits because she loves you and wants what's best for you."

Emmy met his blue eyes that were dimming with age. "Josh is what's best for me."

Uncle Carl nodded. "I trust your judgment, Darlin'."

He patted her arm before turning to the car.

"Sorry you drove all this way," she said.

He turned back with a smile. "It was a nice drive up. We'll see how the drive home goes." He winked. "Give her a few weeks. She'll be thrilled for you when she sees you're happy."

Emmy nodded, wishing she could understand her aunt the way her uncle did.

Uncle Carl took his time getting to the car, waving goodbye to them as he drove away. Jalina stared straight ahead but Emmy could see her mouth moving. Poor Uncle Carl.

She turned to Josh. "I'm sorry. She's...a piece of work."

He swallowed and studied the grass. "She's probably right, you know. I never could provide for you like Grayson did and there is a huge gap in our social status."

Emmy grabbed his chin with her hand, and forced him to meet her gaze. "You look at me and listen to every word I say."

Josh's eyes widened.

"I couldn't care less about how much money you make. I told you how I grew up. What would make you think I give any credence to money or social status?"

Josh glanced at her house.

Emmy released him and wrapped her arms around herself. "I can't believe you think that low of me."

"Whoa." Josh gently tugged her arms open and wrapped her up in a hug. "It's not you I think low of, it's me. I'm just struggling to feel worthy of you."

Emmy leaned into him, careful to avoid his stitches. "Oh, Josh. You are more than worthy of me." She went on tiptoes and kissed him softly. "Please don't let something as silly as money come between us."

He studied her for a few seconds before slowly nodding. "I don't want anything to come between us."

"Now that sounds more like it." She tangled her fingers in his hair and kissed him again.

Josh chuckled against her lips before wholeheartedly returning the kiss.

"Stop the PDA! You're killing me here!"

Kelton's loud voice projected throughout the street and pulled them a respectable distance apart. Emmy stayed close to Josh, refusing to leave his side for any amount of embarrassment Kelton might heap on them.

Kelton bounded across the lawn. "Dude! You're such a beast. I heard all about you taking a knife for Emmy."

Josh smiled and offered his hand. "Thanks, Kelton."

"If only I'd been there. I could've tracked that dude down and taken him out. Especially if I would've had my d-pole. That guy would still be in the hospital."

Emmy felt the anger at Aunt Jalina and the fear of her attacker slide away as she listened to Josh and Kelton. She did have people who cared about her and the most important one still had his arm around her.

Chapter Twenty-two

EMMY OUTLINED GRAYSON'S NAME with her fingertip then glanced up at the sunshine filtering through the trees. In all of her visits to the cemetery she couldn't remember one where she hadn't been rained on. She glanced over her shoulder at the police car. The nonstop protection was getting old, but it was nice to feel safe.

She'd finally told Grayson everything about Josh, except for how she felt when she kissed him. "I'm not saying I'm going to get married tomorrow, but I think I'm ready to move on." She grimaced. "I'm sorry. I hate how that sounds, like I'm going to forget you, forget us. You were my best friend, Grayson. I won't forget. I promise."

A ray of sunshine found its way through the branches to Emmy. She closed her eyes and turned her face up. The warmth of it enveloped her like Grayson's kindness and lanky arms used to do. Emmy sat there until the moment passed and the pine trees blocked the sun from her again.

She glanced back at the grave, studying Grayson's likeness. "You're okay with this?"

Emmy felt the same warmth inside of her. She didn't understand how Grayson knew and approved, but he did. He'd always put her happiness first. She knew he'd want her to be happy. "I just feel so guilty." She stopped talking, something inside telling her that the guilt wasn't what Grayson wanted. A laugh bubbled up in her throat. He loved her as much now as he had when he was alive. He loved her enough he was giving her his blessing to move on, to find happiness. With Josh.

She bent down and kissed his picture on the gravestone. "Thank you, love. You'll always be my first."

Chapter Twenty-three

THE DOORBELL RANG. Emmy wasn't expecting anyone and felt the familiar clutch in her abdomen. Why did she have to be terrified all the time? Why couldn't the police find the guy?

The doorbell rang again.

She picked her phone off the counter and cautiously approached the front door. She knew it wasn't Josh as she'd told him she would bring dinner to his house. She'd been grating some parmesan to put on the chicken and mushroom baked pasta. She could hardly wait to take the food over and tell him about her experience at the cemetery this afternoon. She got chills just imagining his reaction. She grinned. Good chills.

Double checking the key pad by the front door she saw that the alarm system was on. If anything suspicious happened she could call 911 and hope the police, who always seemed to linger close by, would save her.

Peeking through the sidelight next to the wooden door, she expelled all her breath. "Shane," she called out. "Just give me a second to disable the alarm."

He smiled back through the glass and mouthed his thanks.

Emmy punched in the code, then twisted the deadbolt

and pulled the door open. The sun setting behind her house cast shadows through the neighborhood.

"Hello, Emmy," Shane offered in his soft voice. "I wanted to talk to you about some ideas I had with the stage."

Emmy nodded. He was such a nice person and she'd turned him down so often she didn't want to refuse him now. "Sure, come in." She held the door as he shuffled passed. She glanced around for any of the police cars that constantly patrolled her street but none were visible.

Shane hovered behind her and she slowly pushed the door shut.

"I hope it's okay I came to your house. I was just so excited about the idea."

"Sure. Do you want to sit down?"

He walked slowly to the living room, perching on the edge of the couch. Emmy sat in the overstuffed chair and watched him, hoping he wouldn't be too long so she could finish dinner and get to Josh.

"I think I have a way to do a platform that would raise and lower the Beast for different scenes. I'll design it with a hydraulic lift. It would make such an impact, especially when we use smoke and some fireworks to add to his fearsome visage." He rubbed at his short beard.

Emmy noticed he'd trimmed his hair. He looked really nice. "I love it. What a great idea."

He puffed his chest out, grinning, but then his eyes fell to a picture of her and Grayson on the coffee table. He cleared his throat before rushing out the words, "Would you like to go to dinner and talk about some other ideas I have?"

Emmy bit her lip. "I'm sorry, but I already told you I'm involved with someone else." She pointed to the mess in the kitchen. "I'm making dinner for him right now." Hopefully he'd take the hint and go.

His face slackened. "Is it the firefighter?"

"Yes." Emmy didn't like the sad look in his eyes. Why did he have to keep asking and make her feel like the bully again and again? She stood. "I really love your idea. Thank you for always working so hard for the theater."

Shane covered the distance separating them and grasped her arm, drawing her closer. "You don't understand, Emmy. I don't do it for the theater, I do it for you!"

Emmy's breath quickened. Her phone was on the entryway table. She wanted it in her hand right now. Panic tightened every muscle. "Shane, you're hurting me. Let go of my arm."

He looked down at his fingers on her arm. "Oh, I'm sorry." He released her. "I just really want a chance with you."

Emmy stared into his eyes. They were an odd dark-gray, almost black. She'd never noticed. "Shane. You need to stop pursuing me. You're a very nice person and I'm sure someday you'll find someone who will be perfect for you."

Shane shook his head and moved closer, towering over her. "But I want you."

Emmy needed to run. She kept breathing in and out to stay calm and wait for the right opportunity. Why was Shane acting like this? Was he the one who had sent the notes and killed Grayson? It would have been so easy for him working behind the scenes at the theater to slip the notes in at different times. The police had cleared him after the murder but she knew Shane was smart. Had he outsmarted all of them? Her heart thumped against her rib cage. She gripped the couch for support as her thoughts turned desperate. How was she going to escape?

Someone pounded on the front door and shouted, "Emmy! Open up!"

Emmy scurried around Shane, who looked like a lost puppy in a rainstorm, and hurried to the front door. She flung it open, praying it was Josh.

"Timothy?"

His dark eyes glinted dangerously as he strode in and pushed her behind him, shutting the door with his other hand. "Did he hurt you?"

"No." She shook her head, relieved and confused. "How did you know to come?"

"I've been wondering if he was the murderer and I followed him tonight."

Shane hadn't moved from the living room. He stared at the two of them as if in a daze. Timothy kept his voice low, his arm in front of her as if shielding her. "He killed Grayson and I just found Josh...he's dead."

Emmy sagged against Timothy's back. "No." Everything darkened as happiness was sucked from her life.

"I knew Shane was interested in you. I wondered if he might be the murderer. I started tracking him. I got to Josh's just as his car pulled away. I'm so sorry."

"No!" He'd taken Grayson. He couldn't take Josh.

Her vision clouded. The room swayed. Sadness consumed her but was quickly replaced by fury. The anger built within Emmy until she wanted to explode. She ducked under Timothy's arm and flew across the wooden floor. She went after Shane with both fists, banging against his face. "How could you? How could you?"

Shane grabbed at her arms to protect himself. "What did I do?"

Timothy came from behind, wrapping his gloved hands around her and pulling her several steps away. "Stay away from her," he commanded Shane.

Shane moved toward them. "You're the one who should stay away from her."

Timothy shoved Emmy to the ground, yanked a black pistol from his jacket pocket, and fired. Shane slammed against the back of the couch and slid to his knees. His face filled with shock as his hand went to the blood stain blossoming on his chest. He whispered, "Emmy," and slumped over.

"Shane!" Emmy screamed. She crawled to him, feeling for a sign of life. Blood streamed down his shirt. He still had a pulse but it was faint. She looked up at Timothy. "You shot him!"

He stared down at her like she was nuts. "He killed your husband, Emmy. He killed Josh. He was coming after you. It was self-defense."

Emmy's breath came hard and fast. She couldn't think straight. Josh couldn't really be dead. Timothy couldn't have just shot Shane. She needed help. She needed Josh. Wouldn't she feel it if he was gone? A sob wrenched from her chest. Probably not. She'd had no clue when Grayson died. Shadows pressed in on her. Her entire world was crumbling. She had no one. Nothing. She'd barely started to heal from Grayson's death. She would never heal from Josh's.

Timothy lifted her up and pressed her head into his chest. "It's okay, Love. I'll take care of everything."

Emmy shook her head in confusion. This was Timothy. Her friend. Why was he calling her love? How could he have just shot Shane?

"I'm going to call the police and they will take care of everything. Stay here while I go check on Josh."

"Stay *here?*"

"Listen to me. I know you were developing feelings for Josh. I don't want you to see..."

The tears slid out then. She trembled and tried to swallow away the dryness in her throat and the aching emptiness in her heart.

"I'm so sorry he did this to you, but I'll take care of everything, my love."

Emmy stared up at him. "Why do you keep saying that? You said I was like a sister to you."

Timothy smiled gently, brushing a lock of hair from her face with a gloved finger. "I lied. I knew you were falling for Josh, and I didn't want to get in the way of your happiness. I didn't know that Shane was the murderer, but now he's killed Josh and I want to take care of you, see if you can develop feelings for me."

He released her and set her on a barstool. "Wait here. I've got to get a hold of the police and check on...I'll be right back. I promise."

Emmy blinked back the tears that still wanted to surface. She didn't want to sit here and wait. She wanted to run to Josh's house and discover that somehow he'd survived. But could she handle seeing him cut apart like Grayson? She sat in a daze, staring at Shane's inert form as Timothy hurried out the front door. Her mind couldn't grasp it all. Shane, a murderer, dying in her living room? Josh dead? She pressed a fist to her mouth to hold back the sob.

A groan came from the living room. She glanced at Shane slumped over to the side, blood dripping from his wound.

Creeping to his side, she checked his pulse one more time. It was still there.

She hated him for killing the men she loved, but she couldn't just leave him and hope the EMTs got here soon enough to help. She grabbed a clean kitchen towel and pressed it into the wound on his chest.

"Emmy," he whispered. His eyes opened slightly.

She jumped and scuttled away from him.

"I didn't...kill Grayson," he gasped for air, "or Josh." His eyes closed and he breathed irregularly, the air sounding like a bag of marbles being shaken.

Emmy stared at him. Was he lying? Could Josh still be alive? She stood and grabbed the cordless off her counter. No dial tone. What in the world? She ran to the entryway to get her cell. It was gone.

Emmy glanced back at Shane, shaking her head in confusion. She looked at the front door. Where was Timothy? She ran to the garage and slipped her feet into some Bobs before jumping into the rental car. The keys were gone. Seriously! Timothy had to have taken her keys and her phone. Would he have cut the phone line too? Why? Because he wanted her to wait for him or because...

The air sucked into her lungs then exploded in a strangled scream. She shoved open the car door, pushed the garage button, and sprinted down the street toward Josh's house.

Chapter Twenty-four

JOSH SCRATCHED AT THE STITCHES on his abdomen. He'd stopped taking the pain meds, and the incisions seemed to throb with each heartbeat. He set down the book he was reading and strode to the bathroom. Running his hand over his three-day beard, he frowned. He looked awful. Emmy was bringing dinner at seven. He could shave and give himself a sponge bath so he wouldn't smell like he'd been lying in bed for two days.

He smiled as he thought of how sweet she'd been when she brought dinner two nights ago and the way she'd stood up to her aunt yesterday afternoon. She was amazing. He knew it would be hard to move on and make everything work with her mourning over her husband and her distrust of their "sparks," but he had a lot of hope that they could.

The doorbell rang. He grinned at the thought that Emmy might be early, then grimaced. Quickly splashing some water on his face and brushing his teeth, he grabbed a clean shirt from his room, tugged it carefully over his stitches, and hurried to the living room.

He opened the door and stared at a tall man on his porch. It was the guy who acted with Emmy.

"Hi, we've never been properly introduced. Timothy

White. I perform with Emmy." He gave him a friendly smile but oddly kept his hands in the pockets of his jackets.

Josh nodded. "Josh Campbell."

"Can I come in? I'm concerned about Emmy, and I know you care about her. I wondered if we could talk."

"Sure." Josh stepped back. Timothy sauntered into the house. Josh closed the door, wondering what in the world this man wanted to tell him about Emmy.

Emmy ran like she'd never ran in her life. She saw an old man out watering his gardenias. She stopped long enough to scream at him. "Call 911! There's a man who's been shot at 250 Nebesna Street. Then tell them to go to Josh Campbell's house."

Emmy gasped for air as the man stared at her for a second then repeated, "250 Nebesna?"

"And Josh Campbell."

He nodded and turned toward his house.

Emmy took off at a sprint again. If her instincts were right, she had no time to wait for the police. She just prayed the man would remember the address and name. Hopefully the ambulance could get to Shane before he bled out and she could get to Josh before Timothy killed him.

Chapter Twenty-five

JOSH STUDIED THE MAN SEATED a little too close to him on the couch. He was charismatic and friendly. He explained how happy he was to see Emmy in love again but he was worried because she was over-working herself. He hoped Josh would help her see reason and turn some of the burden of the theater over to him. It was all very thoughtful of the guy, but why did his eyes keep wandering to the picture window, and why didn't he take his hands out of his pockets?

The only thing they knew about the murderer was he was tall and had dark eyes. Timothy was close to Josh's own 6'2". Could this man who appeared so concerned be the one who sliced Josh open the other night? The police had cleared the theater crowd last year, but Timothy could've been smart enough to hide the evidence.

Josh stood and walked a few steps away. "You know I'd love to talk to Emmy any time." He grinned knowingly. If he was right about Timothy, the man was insanely jealous where Emmy was concerned and would lash out if he pushed far enough. "It might take some convincing, if you know what I mean." He pumped his eyebrows. "But I'm sure I could *help* her see reason."

Timothy's mouth tightened. He stood, coming closer to Josh. "I'd appreciate that." He gave Josh a forced smile.

The door burst open. Emmy flung herself into the room, her dark hair sticking up crazily and sweat pouring down her face as she screamed, "Josh!"

Josh stared at her before the glint of metal took his attention. He jumped backward, his shoulder slamming into the wall.

"Timothy, no!" She stepped forward, her hands out.

Timothy had a long knife in his gloved hands and a wicked grin on his face. "Shut the door, Emmy, or I'll kill him right now."

Emmy did as instructed but the look in her eyes was pure hatred. "You killed Grayson!"

"You and I were meant to be together." He kept the knife and his attention on Josh as he spoke soothingly to Emmy. "The first time I heard you sing I knew it, and the chemistry between us when we act is amazing. You're the first woman who didn't come to me, so I had to be patient."

"Patient? You killed my husband!"

"You weren't good together." He waved the knife dismissively.

"I loved him!"

He snorted. "Only because you're so good. He wasn't worthy of you and you weren't compatible." He looked back at her and winked. "You and I, we're going to be wonderful together."

Josh's stomach rolled. This man would never be with Emmy; he didn't care what kind of weapons Timothy threw at him.

"It was you sending the notes all along?" Emmy asked.

Josh understood that Emmy wanted to have her questions answered, but right now he just wanted to disarm the guy. If she could keep him talking maybe he could jump in and push the knife away.

Timothy seemed to sense Josh's focus and looked at him, moving a few inches closer. "Yes. I wanted you to see you could leave your husband and I would be there for you." He shrugged. "When you didn't leave him, I decided to open your options further."

She clenched her fists and a tear trickled down her cheek. Josh wished he could go to her, but there wasn't enough room to get around Timothy without getting cut, or worse. He tried to slide to the left, but Timothy followed his movement.

"You murdered him."

"I know what I did." He laughed. "And he was so stupid, thought you'd invited me in. Asked me to sit down and watch golf. I didn't enjoy killing him, but I knew when I'd been handed the perfect opportunity."

Emmy flinched, her chest rising and falling quickly.

"Then after he died I gave you time to heal. I gave you time to trust me, to see that I would be good for you." His face hardened and he glared at Josh. "And you moved on to your fireman."

"But why kill Shane?"

"Think, Love. I've been working the Shane angle for a while now. I knew everyone would believe that weirdo would stalk you so I followed you at the cemetery and crept around your porch to make it more believable. I got impatient and decided to kidnap you the night I sliced him open," he glared at Josh, "but I'm glad I didn't because tonight everything worked out. I left a note that you killed Shane because he killed Grayson and Josh. Your fingerprints are all over him and I planted the gun in your kitchen drawer." He held up a gloved hand. "Not a print of mine on him. Then I got Shane's fingerprints on the same knife that killed Grayson and once I kill Josh, we'll leave together. It's perfect."

"Not so perfect." Emmy laughed derisively. "Shane isn't dead and the police are on their way."

Timothy flinched but didn't take his eyes off of Josh. "The police are all investigating a robbery at Mo's. But I'll carve you up quick so Emmy and I can be on our way. Emmy's got enough money for us to go anywhere we want."

Josh's stomach flinched remembering the pain this blade had already created. He grabbed a heavy firefighting award off the coffee table to his right and chucked it. The trophy caught Timothy in the stomach. He grunted, but kept coming with the knife.

Emmy crossed the room in a blur and jumped onto Timothy's back, pounding at him and screaming, "You won't hurt him!"

"Emmy! No!" Josh yelled. The entire ugly scene slowed down as Timothy flicked the knife back, ripping through Emmy's shirt and into the flesh of her back. Her scream of anguish tore at Josh worse than Timothy's blade had the other night.

Emmy fell to the ground in a heap, her eyes wide as she pressed her fingers into the blood oozing down her back.

"You made me hurt her!" Timothy raged, diving at Josh.

The knife flashed toward his face. Josh ducked under the blade and slammed his fist into Timothy's wrist, hearing a satisfying crunch. Timothy dropped the knife and squealed.

Josh grabbed Timothy's injured arm, twisted it behind him, and forced him to the ground, causing more screaming. Josh slammed Timothy's head into the wood floor. He wrapped the crook of his elbow around the man's throat and latched his other hand on his own forearm. He pulled for all he was worth. Timothy struggled—thrashing, kicking, and screaming obscenities until he thankfully passed out.

Josh jumped off him and rushed to Emmy. "Oh, Em," he moaned. He crossed her body so that he could keep Timothy in his line of site while he took care of her.

She looked up at him, tears running down her cheeks. "You're okay."

"*I'm* okay?" His breath rushed out. He lifted her tattered shirt, examining the wound. It was long but didn't look as deep as he had feared. Josh whipped his shirt off, ignoring the pull on tender flesh as one of the stiches caught. He pressed the clean shirt against her wound with his left hand while fishing his cell phone out with his right. He dialed 911 then rested the phone against his ear so he could put more pressure on the wound with his right hand. Emmy winced. He wished he didn't have to add to her pain, but he had to stop the blood flow.

"Emmy, you've been sliced open. Who cares if I'm okay?"

She craned her neck and lifted his chin so he was looking directly at her. "I do," she whispered.

Chapter Twenty-six

AFTER ENDURING FAR TOO MANY QUESTIONS from the police in a private room at the hospital, Josh and Emmy were able to check on Shane. He was still in the ICU, but in stable condition. The bullet pierced his right lung, thankfully missing other vital organs. He was in for a lot of surgery and a long recovery, but they were hopeful. Timothy's wrist was cast and he was taken into police custody. They assured Emmy the trial would be quick and he would be locked up for a long, long time.

Emmy had been released into Josh's care after an embarrassingly small amount of stitches. Josh fussed over her like she'd been in a life or death struggle; holding her up as if she couldn't walk on her own and planning every movement to make sure it didn't hurt her.

They left the hospital in Seaside after the staff agreed to keep them updated on Shane's condition. Josh gently assisted her through the dark parking lot and into his truck. She squirmed when her tender back bumped into the seat and tried to hide it from him. He rushed around to the driver's side, a grimace on his face as he climbed in. His injury was healing but was still worse than her little cut.

"Maybe we should drive my car until we're both healed." She smiled. "Easier to get into."

143

Josh chuckled. "As long as we're together, I don't care what we drive."

Emmy loved the idea of driving everywhere together. "Sure you don't. I know your type. You love being in your sweet, pimped-out big rig."

His chuckle turned into a long laugh. "*Pimped*-out? Yeah, that sounds just like me." He shook his head. "Where to?"

She leaned her shoulder against the leather to stare at his handsome profile and keep her wound from rubbing against the seat. "I'm starving."

"Me too. I was waiting for an amazing dinner and instead I got another knife fight and half a night in the hospital. What sounds good?"

She glanced at the green time display: 1:30 a.m. "I don't know that we have a lot of options."

"McDonalds is just down the street."

Emmy cringed. "I must be really hungry. I think I can stomach McDonald's."

"Or I could cook for you. Eggs or mac and cheese?"

"McDonald's it is."

Emmy was exhausted and ready to lie down, but being with Josh for a while longer was worth it. After they got their food and were driving back to Cannon Beach, Emmy asked, "Do you want to come to my house and eat?"

He winked. "I thought you'd never ask."

The drive went quickly and before long she was punching in the code at her garage. A strange sensation passed over her as they walked into her house and flipped on lights. Freedom. She was free from the guilt of betraying Grayson. She was free from the fear of not knowing who or where the murderer was. She was free to pursue a life with Josh.

She glanced around at her clean house. One of Josh's police buddies told her at the hospital that after they'd cleared the crime scene, Kelton's family had come and scrubbed everything. She'd have to make them a basketful of treats.

Josh set the food on the counter. He turned to her with a smile. "Are you going to share your fries with me?"

Emmy ran her fingers over the muscles of his shoulder. "And more."

Josh's eyebrows elevated and then his smile grew. "Really?"

She made the mistake of lifting her right hand and felt the pain run down her back. She ignored it and pulled him closer with her left hand. Her mouth found his like a magnet drew them together. The sparks were flying as she showed him without words how much she wanted to be with him. She finally pulled away and looked shyly at him through her lashes.

"I thought you were hungry," Josh said, "but wow."

Emmy bit her lip. "I was definitely hungry." She sat at the bar. "We should probably eat this grease before it gets cold and really disgusting."

Josh grinned. "Okay. But we're eating quick."

Emmy quivered with warmth and anticipation. She opened her Big Mac and took a small bite. It tasted better than she remembered.

Josh ate two Double Stacks, an order of chicken nuggets, and half her fries before she'd finished her sandwich. He quickly cleaned up the trash then helped her from her seat. "Come on. Let's get you comfortable."

Escorting her to the couch, he settled her lying on her side with pillows and a soft blanket he had retrieved from her bedroom. He sat on the floor and rested a hand at her waist.

"Do you care if I stay here and watch you sleep?"

Emmy smiled, too tired to protest much. "You need to sleep too."

Josh nodded. "After you fall asleep, I'll make a bed on the floor."

"But I want you to be comfortable."

His grin revealed his dimples. "Oh, I will be."

"I love your dimples." She stroked her hand along his cheek.

"Dimples?" He looked properly affronted. "I don't have dimples."

"Yes, you do. But only when you really smile."

He shook his head. "I think you're making it up."

"Maybe you only really smile for me."

"Now that is the truth." He gave her a gentle kiss then leaned back on his haunches to study her.

She didn't want to close her eyes, but his handsome face was growing fuzzy. Emmy had only let them give her a local anesthetic, but the night had drained her. She couldn't fight the exhaustion anymore. "Josh."

"Yes?"

"I am."

"What?"

"You wanted me to be comfortable." She reached out a hand and he took it. His touch made her stomach flutter. "I'm comfortable with you. And you're also right—the sparks will still be there in fifty years."

They sat smiling at each other until Emmy couldn't keep her eyes pried open any longer.

The wonderful smell of onions, peppers, ham, and other

things sizzling brought Emmy out of her comatose state. She managed to push herself up on the sofa until she could see Josh cooking in her kitchen. Tingles spread from her scalp to her toes. His long hair was slightly wet. He wore a clean T-shirt and jeans, pushing food around in a pan. When had he run home and showered?

"Good morning," she croaked.

Josh glanced up and grinned. "It is." He studied her for several seconds until Emmy flushed. Her hair was frizzing everywhere and her breath tasted like rotten hamburger. "Hungry?" he asked.

"I thought you said you could only cook eggs."

"Yeah. But I can put a lot of stuff in the eggs."

"It smells wonderful." She stood, slowly straightening. The pain wasn't bad. Thank heavens the cut was superficial. "Excuse me for a minute."

Josh started forward. "Do you need help?"

"No!"

He jerked back.

"Sorry. No. I just need to use the restroom."

He nodded. "Oh, guess I shouldn't help with that."

"Only over my physically-incapacitated body."

He shook his head and turned back to the frying pan. "Life is always going to be fun with you."

"You hope," she flung at him as she walked away.

"Yes, I do." He winked.

Emmy couldn't hide her smile as she gingerly climbed the stairs. She wished she could shower, but instead settled for a change of clothes, washing with a washcloth, and applying some makeup. With freshly brushed teeth, she descended the stairs, excited to see what the day with Josh would bring.

Josh had two plates of food set out next to milk and orange juice. The eggs didn't look spectacular but they tasted great. After breakfast, Josh insisted on cleaning up. Emmy brushed her teeth again, applied some peppermint lip gloss, and waited for him on the back patio.

She leaned on her railing and watched the sun reflect off the water. Seagulls floated in the wind above a young couple strolling the waterline. The peace and beauty of it almost made her cry. She hadn't realized how much she'd truly missed the simple things like sitting on her porch without worrying if someone would hurt her.

Josh opened the door behind her. Turning, she smiled. His blue eyes were lit with love and happiness.

"Do you feel it?" she asked.

He carefully wrapped his arms around her back, avoiding her injury. "What's that?"

"The pull between us?"

He bent to kiss her lightly then raised his head to look into her eyes. She had been semi-joking, but the pull she felt at that moment was no laughing matter. His head descended again and her fears of the past year melted away as she lost herself in his kiss and the passion and love she felt for him.

"Yes, I feel it," he whispered against her lips.

Emmy leaned her head against his shoulder. "I didn't realize how terrified and lonely I've been. My world got smaller and smaller over the last year, trapping me in a bubble of fear. Now it's like I have everything in the world. Peace, happiness, you."

He tilted her head up so she looked into his eyes. "You definitely have me, and I will do everything in my power to keep you safe and happy."

"I know you will." She took a deep breath, hoping she wouldn't ruin the moment but needing to tell him. "I went to the cemetery yesterday."

He cleared his throat, suddenly looking like a teenager asking for his first dance. "And?"

"And Grayson gave us his blessing." She nodded. "I'm ready to move on. I can be happy and not feel like I'm hurting Grayson."

Josh sucked in a breath. Emmy knew she must be crazy because it looked like his eyes were glistening. "He's a better man than me, Em. I don't know if I could ever give you my blessing to be with someone else."

"Oh, Josh." Emmy found she was fighting tears herself. "There could never be someone else after you."

He swallowed and shook his head. "I love you, Em. And if something ever happened to me, I would want you to be happy."

Emmy shook her head. "Don't you ever talk about something happening to you. Ever! You got that?"

Josh half-laughed. "Okay, I won't. But I'm serious."

Emmy kissed him for several long minutes, her salty tears mingling with the warmth of his lips. "I know you are. And don't you ever say anyone's a better man than you. I love you, and no one is a better man than you. No one."

Josh groaned and pulled her closer. His kiss had her clinging to him and moving in ways that weren't smart with stitches. She ignored the pain and enjoyed each touch.

"Sorry to be such a wimp, but could you say it one more time?"

She glanced up at him. "What?"

He laughed. "Come on. I'm supposed to be a tough guy. Don't make me beg."

"Okay. You first."

"That's easy." He kissed her softly. "I love you, Emmaline Henderson. I'll love you until the day I die."

Emmy smiled so hard her cheeks ached. "I love you, Joshua Campbell. I'll love you even when I'm in heaven."

"I knew you were a one-up kind of girl."

Emmy shrugged. "You're going to know a lot of things about me."

"Yes, I am." Josh kissed her again and Emmy knew it was going to be a lot of fun sharing all of those things.

About the Author

CAMI CHECKETTS IS A WIFE to a daredevil husband; a mother to four future WWF champions; an exercise scientist trying to make her corner of the world healthier; and a writer hoping for more time to write.

Please refer to her website – http://www.camichecketts.com for more information about her books. For fitness articles and exercise advice – http://fitnessformom.blogspot.com

Other books by Cami:

The Broken Path
Fourth of July
Dead Running
Dying to Run
Running Home
Poison Me
Blog This
The Colony

If you enjoyed *Shadows in the Curtain* please consider posting a review on Amazon, Goodreads, or your personal blog. Thank you for helping to spread the word.

A portion of the proceeds from *Shadows in the Curtain* will be donated to The Child and Family Support Center. For more information on this worthy cause – www.cachecfsc.org

Sign up for Cami's newsletter here.

www.camichecketts.com

Excerpt from

BLOG *This*

By Cami Checketts

Chapter One

ALEX CLUTCHED THE SCRAP OF PAPER between cold fingers, checking the address for the third time. Had he misunderstood? He glanced around the upscale neighborhood and then focused on the redbrick two story, its wide front porch decorated with monstrous stone pillars. The porch was cleared of snow and free from garbage. Not a typical dwelling for one of his assignments.

Happy chattering, punctuated with giggles and shouts, drifted to him from the backyard. Crunching through knee-deep snow, Alex rounded the edge of the home and viewed the target for the first time. His gut twisted. He'd known the target was a mother, but hadn't let himself dwell on that detail.

He watched the woman for several seconds, unable to draw a full breath. The petite redhead was beautiful and obviously enjoying herself, an attractive combination. She bent and fastened a snowboard to her boots. Her son laughed at something she said. The corners of her eyes and mouth crinkled as she smiled back. They were the image of bliss—an ideal Alex had never experienced.

The woman's little girl patted the snow, red curls bouncing as she played. There was something off about the child, the shape of her eyes and the way she appeared to babble rather than talk. Alex's throat constricted. He groaned as his own little sister's face materialized. The similarities were unmistakable. No. He would not kill this child's mother.

Alex retreated, stumbling over the snow. He jerked the cell phone from his pocket and dialed with trembling fingers. His hip slammed into the driver's side door of the rented Avalon before the call connected.

"Are you sure?" he asked, standing next to the car with his palm still on the door handle.

"About what?"

He rattled off the address and a description of the young mother, wondering if the churning of his stomach was audible through the phone line. "I have the right target?"

"Yes."

"She has children." He shivered, a chilly wind counteracting the sweat beading on his forehead. "They look . . ." He paused.

"Look what?"

"Happy." Alex shuffled his foot through a spot of slush

on the driveway, trying to find a way to explain himself to a man who equated happiness with more money and power. "The little girl—"

"I don't care if the happy mama is running an orphanage full of sunshine. She's hurting my sales, again, and this time she's got some lobbyists believing her garbage. If she ruins my chance for this contract." He cursed. "I don't want to think about this woman anymore. Take care of her and get to the airport. I need my plane back."

"But the little girl." Alex cleared his throat. "She has Down syndrome."

"Save it, Alex. She's not Anna." A heavy exhale came through the phone. "Finish the job. Is some kid you don't know worth more than your own sister?"

Sweat drenched Alex's chest. Bile reached the top of his throat. His puppeteer didn't make hollow threats, and Alex always executed perfectly because the man knew how to keep him performing.

"This isn't right." Alex thought of the other hits he'd done, usually male, their clothing worth more than their contribution to society. His boss had many enemies and didn't hesitate to eliminate any who offended him or threatened his success. This woman had done both.

"Don't question me. Take care of the woman and get my plane back or *I'll* visit Anna."

Alex clenched a fist. Someday soon he would do a lot more than question, but he needed time—time to save more money so he and Anna could disappear, time to study the facility where Anna was being held, and time to break her out without endangering her.

The threat held for several seconds before Alex admitted to himself that he had no choice. "Okay," he muttered.

"What was that?"

"It's done." He couldn't risk Anna's safety. He disconnected the phone, shoved his compassion into the snow, and fingered the gun concealed in his jacket.

Forcing his legs into a trot, Alex descended upon the target's private world. Fury clouded his vision. He hated his boss and everything the man demanded of him, but he had to wonder who was the bigger coward—the man blackmailing him, or the man who faithfully pulled the trigger.

Chapter Two

NATASHA SENECOT WOBBLED TO A STOP at the base of the snow-covered hill. She jabbed her fist into the air, glancing up the incline at her children. "*Yes!* I did it." Jumping off the snowboard, she shimmied a quick victory dance before hoisting the board and hiking to the top of the slope.

Her son, Jace, pounded his gloved hands together. "Woo-hoo, Mom. After like a million crashes, you didn't fall."

"Almost forgot about those." Natasha set the snowboard down and flipped her hair off her neck. "I am a *snowboarder*." She scooped two-year old Lily off the ground and stole the mitten from her mouth.

"Hey-a," Lily issued a stream of unintelligible commands, pointing to the mitten.

Natasha nodded along with each word and replaced the glove. "It's an accessory, not an appetizer." She grinned and rubbed noses with her daughter. "How come you're so cute?"

Lily's smile widened.

Natasha rested Lily on her hip, turned to Jace, and pointed down the slope that formed the western border of their backyard. "That is a big hill. You have a right to be proud of your old mama."

"You're *so* old." Jace laughed, rattling the dark spikes on his head. "Big hill, my bum. Give me my board. I'll show you how a ninja conquers the snow."

"Go, ninja!"

Lily giggled at her mom's cheering. Natasha nudged the

snowboard with the toe of her boot, watching her nine-year old slip on the footholds without sizing down the bindings. His feet were almost the same size as hers; he would be tall like his dad. *Tony.* Thoughts of her ex-husband filled her with a familiar longing. She shook her head, refusing to let herself drool over something that was lost.

Jace leaned forward and wove expertly down the mound.

"Lovin' the ninja snowboarder," Natasha called, the grin she'd lost moments ago creeping back onto her face. "Are you having fun, cutes?" She kissed Lily's cheek, inhaling the warmth of baby lotion.

"Offa." Lily yanked at her Dora hat.

"No." Natasha squinted at the hills west of her neighborhood that intersected the Wellsville Mountains. The sun glistened off heaps of snow but the temperature was above forty today—a blessed reprieve from the inversions they normally endured in their northern Utah valley. The tree boughs, unburdened of their icy coat, saturated the air with the scent of pine.

Lily squirmed, tugging at her glove. "Offa, offa."

"No way, cutes." Natasha pressed the mitten back into position. The kids had succeeded in wriggling out of their coats a few minutes ago, but Natasha insisted that Lily keep her hat and gloves on. She didn't know if it was because Lily was born with Down syndrome, but her baby seemed to snag every illness that traveled through wind, snot, or saliva.

Jace trudged to the top of the hill and dug the board into the snow. "Your turn, Mom. Don't biff it." He opened his hands for his sister. "C'mere, Lils. Mommy's going to fall off the snowboard."

Natasha handed him Lily. "After weeks of painful

crashes, I am now *the* expert snowboarder." She rubbed at the latest bruise on her backside.

Jace laughed. Setting Lily on her feet, he steadied her with both hands under her armpits. "One good slide don't prove nothin'." Jace sat on the snow and tugged Lily down next to him. He leaned toward his sister's ear and said in a stage whisper, "Help me make snowballs. We'll throw them at Mommy when she crashes."

Lily giggled as if she understood and followed her brother's example. Together, they dug into the crusty snow to assemble their arsenal.

"*If* I crash." Natasha pried open the plastic bindings of the cheap snowboard Jace had received from Santa last month and slid her flowered Bogs into position. The descent shouldn't even be classified as a hill, but she still managed to gain new sore spots on most runs. She leaned forward. The tip plunged off the edge and she flew toward the bottom. Her stomach hopped. Cool air brushed her cheeks. *This is great. When I don't crash.*

Without warning, the glossy surface gained the advantage. The board slid out from under her feet. Natasha's rear banged onto the ice and scooted to a stop. "Oomph," she grunted, pain radiating up through her back. A new bruise would appear tomorrow. She watched the snowboard finish its journey across the yard, minus its rider.

"You suck," Jace yelled.

"Watch it. I raised you with a better vocabulary than that."

He laughed. "Your awful crashes are amazing."

It wasn't poetic, but he was only nine. "If you weren't making fun of me, I'd be impressed." Natasha laid back in the snow, resting her eyes and smiling to herself. She did suck, but she didn't care—this was quality time they didn't often get. She relaxed, enjoying the contrast of warm sweat rolling down her back and the cold seeping through her sweatshirt.

Jace's laughter stopped suddenly. An unnatural quiet descended upon the yard. Natasha forced her eyelids open, squinting against the brilliance of the sun.

"Mom!"

Natasha sat up. The world swam for a second. Jace and Lily were still perched on the hill above her. Lily happily patted the snow, but Jace's face was pinched. He pointed toward the barren lilacs extending from the north end of the house to the neighbor's fence. Natasha focused on the source of his distress. A tall figure studied them through the bushes.

Who is that? Natasha scrambled to her feet. Her heartbeat escalated.

The man strode toward her, stopping less than ten feet away. He glared down, towering over her 5'4". Dark bristles covered the lower half of his face. His pale features were model perfect, long lashes showcasing black licorice eyes. His face gave no hint as to why he'd invaded their privacy.

Tearing her eyes from him, Natasha glanced at her children. Jace didn't speak or move. Lily screamed her version of hello. The man didn't answer. Natasha pivoted back to face him, unsure why she felt such a strong urge to scream for help and run to protect her children.

His gaze locked on hers. His eyes were so cold. A chill wind swept over her, but the branches on the trees didn't move.

"Can I help you?" She clutched her gloved fingers to stop the trembling.

His eyes darkened. His lips stayed in a tight line.

"Did you, um, get lost?" Natasha forced an unsteady laugh and arched her eyebrows. "Easy to do in a town of less than three thousand people." He didn't crack a smile so she released her own, pointed toward the front yard, and stiffly recited driving directions. "Highway 89 is less than a mile east of here. The fastest route is to drive straight out of the neighborhood and then take two-hundred s-s..."

His right arm rose—a black pistol molded to his palm. Heart thudding, Natasha's voice sputtered and died. She raised her hands and backed up a few steps. Her gaze darted to Jace and Lily.

"Mom!" Jace pulled Lily against his side.

Natasha felt colder than the snow clinging to her boots. The only lucid thought she had was the overwhelming need to protect Jace and Lily. *I have to say something, do something.* "Please, please don't hurt us."

The lines in his face hardened, anger seeping from his dark gaze. The hand holding the gun remained steady.

Natasha's mind raced, trying to comprehend a man pointing a gun at her with Jace and Lily feet away. Was there any way to keep them safe?

"Look," she began, her voice trembling on each word, "I-I've got some cash in the house. I can give you my credit card and the pin numbers for my debit card. The credit card has a hundred-thousand dollar limit." It was a lie, but might buy her children's safety.

He shook his head. "I'm not after your money." His voice was barely above a rough whisper.

Her stomach dove. Sweat formed on her palms. This couldn't be happening. "I'll give you anything you want." She took a deep breath and lowered her voice. "*Anything*, just please, not in front of my children. We could go in the house and . . ." Her voice trailed off as disgust filled her throat.

She tilted her chin, holding his gaze. *I don't care. Whatever I have to do to keep them safe.* If she lured him away, Jace could run for help and maybe somebody would come before . . . She convulsed at the image of what she had offered. The man outweighed her by at least a hundred pounds, but she wouldn't go down without a fight.

The man's eyes flickered up the hill to Jace and Lily. Lily waved, grinning brightly. Seconds passed. He looked back at Natasha with a scowl. "I don't want that either."

Then why are you here? She cast a nervous glance at her children. Jace clung to Lily, watching his mother bargain for their lives. What else could she do to protect them? Why was this guy pointing a gun at her?

Suddenly, the latest e-mail threats played through her mind.

Stop your blog or I will send someone to stop it.

Is any cause worth dying for?

The corner of the man's lip quivered. His voice dropped. "I am sorry."

Blinking to clear her vision, Natasha wondered if she'd heard him correctly. "Sorry?"

No. She shook her head. *Oh, no.* Realization came like a moldy dishrag snapped in her face. He *was* here to fulfill the threats. His apology. That brief flicker of regret in his eyes. This man had been sent by Matthew Chrysler to kill her.

"I'll stop the blog."

He shook his head once. "It's too late."

Too late. It was over for her. She didn't want to die, didn't want to leave her family.

Natasha's eyes narrowed and her lips compressed. He could kill her, but no way was he going to hurt her children. She glanced over her shoulder at Jace. "Run," she mouthed. "Take Lily." He nodded once, wrapping his arm more securely around Lily's waist.

Natasha focused on the man. His finger hung lazily on the trigger like he had all the time in the world.

"Look," she said. "I'm sure we can work something out."

The word "out" escaped her mouth at the same instant that she pushed off with her left foot and launched herself at the man. One eyebrow rose, but he didn't flinch. She made it two steps before the whoosh of the silenced gun told her she'd lost.

Buy your copy of *Blog This* on Amazon.com

Made in the USA
Middletown, DE
06 August 2023

36301327R00096